THE ARRANGEMENT

KIERSTEN MODGLIN

KIERSTEN
MODGLIN

www.kierstenmodglinauthor.com
Cover Design: Tadpole Designs
Editing: Three Owls Editing
Proofreading: My Brother's Editor
Formatting: Tadpole Designs
First Print Edition: 2021
First Electronic Edition: 2021

To the dream-chasers with messy hair, fire in their souls, and no idea what day it is—
This one's for you.

"Men are afraid that women will laugh at them. Women are afraid that men will kill them."

MARGARET ATWOOD

CHAPTER ONE

AINSLEY

My husband had a tell like no other. When he lied to me, his skin flushed bright red. Not *the slightest blush* red, but *I've just run a marathon* red. It was also the color he became when he was embarrassed.

It was that shade of red I was staring at that night across the dinner table as we discussed our new arrangement.

"So, no questions at all?" he asked, rubbing his thumb over his palm.

"None," I agreed. "It's the only way we can be sure it will work. We aren't accountable to each other for what happens when we're out. We'll each have total freedom."

"Okay." He was breathless, doing everything he could to avoid meeting my eyes.

"But we should have some other rules."

That piqued his curiosity. His gaze found mine.

"Other rules... Like what?"

I tapped my finger against my lips, though I already knew what rules I would require.

"First of all, you can only make connections for your given day. You have Thursdays, I'll do Tuesdays. Every other day of the week, our life has to continue as normal. There are to be no connections made outside of the app at all. We won't give out our phone numbers, no phone calls or texts, etc. And, whoever you're with, whatever you do...protection is a *must*. We'll each need to get tested after every encounter."

"Of course," he said, nodding in agreement.

"This is just for fun, so I think we should also make a rule that we shouldn't see anyone we're immensely attracted to. We don't want either of us to start making genuine connections. It's all physical."

He nodded again, swallowing.

"Okay, yeah. Agreed."

"And the kids can never know," I said, lowering my voice. "As far as they're concerned, nothing can change. You'll be working late on Thursdays, I'll be working late on Tuesdays. Simple as that."

He ran his fingers across his lips.

"Are you sure we can do this?"

I looked down at the table as the sickly feeling washed over me—the one that had been ever-present since the arrangement was proposed a week ago.

"I don't think we have any choice."

"You know I love you, right?" he asked, the tremble in his voice more noticeable than ever.

"I love you too, Peter. This isn't about that. We both agree that things aren't working as they are, and we can either give up and walk away, or we can try something

new." I paused, watching his facial expression harden. "I'm trying here."

"I know. I know you are... I don't want to lose you. Okay," he said, very matter-of-factly. "So when do we start?"

"We can both set up our profiles on the app tonight and start connecting right away." I held up a finger, jaw dropping. "Oh, I almost forgot. I think we should use fake names. It will be easier to keep it all quiet that way. We don't want anyone to find out who we are, or that we're married, or where we work..."

"Yeah, you're right. I like that idea," he said, running his palm over his face.

"Okay, great, so I'll be Annie Green?" I said. A version of my first name and a portion of our last name—Greenburg. "And you can be—"

"Pete Patterson," he answered quickly. Apparently, he'd already given it some thought. "I've always wanted that last name. Like James." He flushed red again as he mentioned his favorite author. I nodded.

"Okay. And we need to make sure we put that we're only looking for something casual. I don't want anyone to get hurt in this process—us or them."

"We're going to end up with a lot of married people doing the same thing, I'd say," he said then laughed. "If only there was an option to just put that as your status."

I didn't laugh with him, because my mind was on whom I might know that may be doing something similar. Somehow, it brought me comfort to know we may not be alone. Maybe we weren't so messed up after all. Maybe others had tried to do this outside of Hollywood movies; maybe they'd had better results than I'd seen depicted in the movies.

That was how the idea was first brought up. During an evening of Netflix last week, we watched the latest sitcom where the couples decided an open marriage was the answer to their problems. We'd seen it a hundred times in a hundred different films or shows, but this time, something sparked inside of me as I watched the wife go out with a stranger.

Peter said some people were crazy.

I said we should try it.

He laughed.

I did not.

And now, a week to the day later, here we were.

It wasn't as if I were some sex-crazed maniac, like some may think. I was simply a woman who loved her husband very much, yet who had been driven to her breaking point. Long ago, sometime between the birth of our first child and the tenth birthday of our third, our marriage fizzled out.

We'd become the cliché couple that you see too often depicted in movies or books. We were boring, *blah*, never touching, rarely talking, both so consumed with work and kids and social media that we didn't have the time or energy to seek out what needed to be fixed.

It wasn't that we hadn't tried. The year before, we'd committed to a date night per week, which was pushed back to a date night per month. It had been seven months at this point since our last one.

Date nights were hard to swing with children at home. Scheduling a sitter weekly added up, cut into family time, and even when we had tried to squeeze in alone time once the kids were asleep, one of us was always too tired or had too much to catch up on.

Two people dedicated to their demanding careers in a stifled marriage made it almost inevitable that problems would soon develop. And we were not immune—problems had arisen in every way.

In the end, I supposed, the cards were stacked against us from every direction. But I was determined not to give up. I was not going to get divorced. I was not going to break up my family and tell my children their father and I would be living apart. We couldn't subject them to a new stepmother and stepfather and all the confusion that came with that. Peter and I had both grown up that way, and we'd agreed years ago to never let it get that bad. But it had.

It was too much. So, this was what we'd come to. This was where we were. Sitting across from each other at our family dinner table, preparing to desecrate our marriage via the wonderful world of online dating—er, I guessed in our case, *online hooking up.*

If I hadn't felt so desperate, I would've been mortified, but it would do no good. I needed to fix this marriage like I fixed so much else in our house and lives, and I'd chosen to move it to the top of the list, above shopping for Maisy's dress for the school dance and behind buying Dylan new cleats for soccer. Our marriage needed to be fixed. And what makes the heart grow fonder quicker than absence? Animal sex with strangers, I had to hope.

I tapped my phone screen, watching it light up. "So, we

set up our profiles and arrange dates. And then next week, we start."

He nodded, rubbing his lips together, his eyes wide. He thought I was trying to trick him, as he would never have expected me to suggest anything this extreme, but he knew me well enough to know I solved problems with an unyielding sword. I was a fixer. Straight to the source. And we needed to be fixed. We'd cut the issues out of our marriage with a few romps in the sack, and then things would be better than ever. I was going to make sure of it. I'd accept nothing less.

"Okay. Well, good luck to you, Annie Green," he said, a small, sad smile playing on his lips as he picked up his phone.

"Good luck, Pete." I reached for his hand, squeezing it as I used my other hand to press the download button on the app that would change our lives.

The app that would fix everything.

I just had to hope it wasn't all a terrible mistake.

CHAPTER TWO

PETER

I hadn't told anyone what we were doing. Not only because I'd promised Ainsley I wouldn't, but also because I was half convinced they wouldn't believe me and half convinced they'd tell me I had it way too good. The truth is, I wasn't sure this *was good*, even as I downloaded the app and filled in my profile information.

Most of the men I knew who used dating apps went with the stereotypical photos of them flexing at the gym and soaked in sweat for their profile pictures. I was of the understanding those photos impressed other men more than they did the women they were trying to woo. Just look at the difference in magazines—Ainsley's magazines were filled with men in sweaters and glasses, smiling in front of a soft-palleted living room. In men's magazines, the men were always ripped, dripping with sweat, angry, and buff. What was the deal? Who were we trying to impress, after all?

I chose a photo of me at work, one that had been taken, but not chosen, for the company profile. I was dressed in a suit and tie, my hair slicked back and neat, with a small, easy smile on my face. It looked like I was saying "Come get to know me. I'm fun and carefree, but also smart and successful." I triple checked the background to be sure there was nothing there that would give away anything personal about myself or my place of work and hit submit.

It was nice enough.

Look, I was never going to win any awards for the most handsome—I had a nice face, a kind smile, but there was nothing spectacular about me. Not like Ainsley. My wife was remarkable, with natural, auburn hair that fell to her mid-back, never a hair out of place unless we were in bed. Her skin was so porcelain I could trace my fingers along her veins when I studied them. She was curved in all the right places, thin in the others. I had no idea girls like her existed outside of dirty magazines and movies until we met.

So, when she suggested we see other people and remain married, my first thought wasn't of the freedom it would give someone like me. Instead, it was of the options it would give someone like her.

Don't get me wrong—I was an average, human, adult male. I had urges and desires and, of course, sleeping with the same woman had gotten old on occasion. Even the most beautiful face gets boring to look at after a while. But that didn't mean I wanted anyone else looking at her. I loved my wife. We'd been through a huge part of our lives together, struggles and triumphs, good times and bad. We'd brought our children into the world side by side. The thought of anyone else getting to spend

time with her, time that should've been mine, was devastating.

Still, I had to agree. I had to accept her conditions because I was worried I'd lose her if I didn't. I knew my wife. I knew once she'd made up her mind about something, there was little that could be done to dissuade her.

Next, I pulled up the section that said 'About Pete' and got to work. I was uninteresting, particularly so because I couldn't mention anything about my job, wife, or children. I was supposed to have done this last night, but I'd been putting it off, trying to describe myself separately from them. Who was I if not a husband, father, and architect? The truth was, I had no idea. So much of my identity was tied up in who they were, who I was to them. I was part of a package, and to separate myself from said package, left me feeling empty and useless.

Ainsley already had a few matches this morning when I checked her phone—I didn't read the messages, I was not a masochist—but it only made it more real for me. We were really going to do this, and I had to get in gear if I wanted to line up a date by Thursday.

I sighed and typed something simple and stupid in the 'About' section.

40. Middle of my class at a university you could care less about.

I should probably put something cool here. So...
Something Cool.

I rolled my eyes, disgusted by the Dad joke, but it was the best I could come up with, which was embarrassing in and of itself. I skipped adding my school but uploaded two more photos, one of me outside after a hike—all the sweat, none of the flexing—and another of me at the beach before I started forming my Dad gut. Best of both worlds there. Men's magazine and women's. In the second picture, there was a beer in my hand, and I wore a care-free smile.

Approachable.

Nice.

I hit *save* and was immediately taken to a screen with a big green button that appeared to be pulsing.

Let's find your match! it said. I allowed my thumb to hover over it briefly before pressing the button and watching it transform into a wheel and begin to spin.

The first profile loaded, bringing a photo to the screen. **Creative!** it said underneath her photo. Was that her name or...? The woman was blonde, younger than me, and she was pretending to laugh in her photo. She seemed cute enough. There were two buttons on my screen: a red heart and a yellow thumbs down. I hit the heart, watched it pulse twice, and then the girl's face disappeared. I waited, wondering what would happen next as a strange sense of excitement bubbled in my stomach.

Instead of being taken to a way to chat with her, another girl's photo filled the screen. She was Black, dressed in a yellow bikini with a genuine smile, and held a glass bottle of beer in her hand. **Adventurous!** I hit the heart button even quicker that time.

The next girl wore hipster glasses and her hair was cut shorter than I would've preferred, but there was some-thing quirky and fun about her. I hit the heart without reservation. There was no reason to be picky, after all, when I wasn't looking for anything serious. I didn't need to connect with anyone, I wasn't trying to build a life with them, I just needed to find them attractive enough to spend an evening with and hope they felt the same way about me. Sudden excitement filled me as I realized I was being presented with a chance to work through every fantasy—every type of woman—I'd ever had any interest in.

A knock on my door caused me to jolt, and I laid the phone down, looking up as Gina stuck her head in my office. "Sorry, am I interrupting something?" She looked as though she'd caught me doing something humiliating. Maybe she had.

"No, sorry. I was texting one of my kids. What's up?"

She laid a stack of papers on my desk, her long brown hair pulled to one side of her shoulders. She pushed the glasses further up on her nose. "Beckman wanted me to bring you this. It's a new proposal for the Cameron development."

I sighed, sliding the phone into the top drawer of my desk as Gina took a seat across from me. "We're thinking the client might approve the budget change if we can get the timeline moved up by two weeks."

I ran a finger under the top page of the proposal, looking it over again. "It'll be tight. We were already pushing it to break ground on the twenty-seventh, but maybe I can call in a few favors."

She grinned with one side of her mouth, her plump lips pushing out as if to say she knew I could do it. Gina was pretty in a sexy librarian sort of way. She wore over-sized sweaters and tight pencil skirts, her hair was usually pulled back into a loose ponytail or bun. She was the kind of woman who could get away with a look like that and somehow still appear corporate and professional.

Other coworkers came in with their blouses and pressed black slacks and still managed to look frumpy compared to her. She'd been a partner at the firm for six years, and up until that moment, I'd been allowed to think such things but never to act on them.

The arrangement Ainsley and I had put into place changed the game in ways I had never even thought of. I forced myself to glance back down at the paper. Getting involved with Gina would be a colossal mistake. She worked with me, and the point of the arrangement was to have casual sex, hang out with people randomly, and, ultimately, use it as a way to once again ignite the fire I'd had with my wife. Getting involved with anyone at the office was strictly forbidden.

"So, you think you can, then?" she asked, filling the silence, and I realized we'd been sitting without saying anything for a long time.

"*Sorry, yeah,*" I blurted out, looking away from her. "I'll call around and see what I can do. If we can do it, the materials may have to be expedited…" I picked up a pencil from the desk, jotting down notes to myself and estimates as I worked through it all in my head. When I looked up, she was watching me curiously. Had she ever looked at me this way before? Not that I could remember. "Everything okay?"

"I was going to ask you the same thing…"

"Yeah, everything's fine here." I chuckled then cleared my throat. "Well, tell Beckman I'll get to work on this and have a definite answer for him by the end of the day."

She rapped her knuckles on the desk, something mischievous in her eyes. Maybe I was giving off some weird pheromone because of my new availability. Was that a thing? "Will do." With that, she stood and walked away from my desk, heading for the door. Normally, I wouldn't allow myself to stare for long, but I was in such a strange new headspace that I gave in to the indulgence.

When she reached the door, she glanced back at me, her cheeks pinkening as she caught me staring. "Call me if you need anything. I'll be in my office," she said, drawing out the words, as if she were waiting for me to say something.

"Thanks, Gina."

With that, she nodded, patting the door with her fingers before she walked from the room. I immediately began to type up an email to our contracting company. My eyes drifted toward the drawer where my phone waited, the allure stronger than I'd expected it would be. I wanted to pull it out, to check it, to browse through the masses of available women again, but I had to pace myself. I had to carry on with my life and make sure I still managed to get work done, too.

I finished the email, adding in the proposed changes to both the budget and timeline, as well as a request that they get back with me before three p.m. I pressed send and glanced back down toward the drawer.

Five minutes.

I'd allow myself five more minutes, and then it was straight back to work.

I checked the clock, as if to enforce it, and opened the drawer. My phone screen was blank, so no matches yet, but had I been expecting anything different? I pressed my thumb to the button that would unlock my phone and opened the app again, brought back to the quirky girl's face. I hit the heart, watching as the next face appeared. The girl appeared to be fake, or if she wasn't, everything about her was. The tiny shirt she was wearing was stretched across her extra-large breasts. Her hair was white-blonde, a stark contradiction to the orange of her tan, bright pink lips, and too-thick eyeliner. I supposed some men might find her attractive, but she seemed to be trying far too hard for me. For the first time, I hit the thumbs down button, almost feeling the need to apologize if she were real.

Within seconds, a new face filled the screen, tearing me away from my guilt, and I swallowed.

What?

Gina's green eyes stared back at me from behind her thick glasses. She had her hair down in the photo, messy and unkempt, a cream-colored oversized sweater hung off one shoulder, and her pale lips were parted slightly.

I stared at the photograph, wondering what to do. It went against all the rules I'd set for myself, but could it have been fate that she was on there? If I hit the heart button, I could explain to her that I was just looking for fun. Maybe she'd be okay with that. I didn't want anything messy, but the woman in the picture didn't look messy at all. She looked uncomplicated. *Fun.*

Maybe I could ease myself into the arrangement by dating someone I knew.

No. Not dating.

Sleeping with.

The thought had my heart racing, my whole body taking notice of the sudden surge of adrenaline.

I stared at the picture a moment longer, wondering what she looked like underneath that sweater. It wasn't as if I hadn't pictured it a million times at that point, but now, I might have the chance to find out.

Without allowing myself to think about it any further, I slid my thumb down the screen and pressed the heart button. It pulsed twice, then to my surprise, instead of disappearing like the others had, it exploded, a swarm of hearts trailing down the screen.

I furrowed my brow.

What the—

The hearts disappeared, revealing a white, nearly blank screen with block lettering in the center.

You've made a match! Click here to connect.

CHAPTER THREE

AINSLEY

When Peter arrived home, I was at the table waiting for him. The kids had disappeared to their respective corners of the home, as was the routine—sometime around their eighth birthdays, they each decided they no longer needed to spend time with us unless absolutely necessary.

The thought crashed into me as I sank into memories of the four of us waiting anxiously for Peter to arrive home from work back then. I remembered the way Dylan and Riley, our oldest boys, would rush toward their father before he could even shut the door, anxious to tell him all about their days. It used to frustrate him. I recalled so vividly him asking that they wait until he'd had a moment to breathe before they pounced on him. If only we'd known how many moments to breathe we'd have as they grew older.

With Maisy, our youngest and only girl, it was different. Peter had always seemed to have time for her, despite the fact that, of all our children, she was the most independent. Perhaps it was because he saw how fast time had gone by with the other two, perhaps it was because she was the easiest child of our three, or perhaps it was because he realized our time was dwindling with our babies in general.

Now, granted, they weren't ready to move out or anything. We still had time with them—Dylan was fourteen, Riley twelve, and Maisy ten. But it seemed like a blink from the time we brought them each home until we had a house of teenagers and preteens. I think the truth was, we'd both realized how quickly time had gotten away from us while we were busy doing other things. How easily we'd let it slip on by. And now, we realized that we had just eight years left, less than Maisy's whole life, which seemed short in comparison to so much else, and then our babies would leave us. They'd be out of the house, on with their lives. And we'd be left with...what?

Our marriage? The one we'd neglected over and over again?

Our home? The one we'd put off repairing in favor of new shoes for the children and extracurriculars?

We had nothing left of what we'd built together in the beginning, and I thought that was what this arrangement had come down to. We needed to decide if there was anything left to fight for.

I didn't want to be the kind of wife in a loveless marriage or the kind of mother who divorced her children's father when the youngest turned eighteen—I knew people like that. They were exhausted—tired and bitter, worn down by a life without romantic love. I didn't want that to be us, but I didn't know what else to do to fix our marriage aside from this. Date nights and random attempts at couples counseling hadn't worked... This was my last resort. If this didn't work, I wasn't sure there was any hope for us. It had to work.

Peter appeared in the doorway of our kitchen, looking worn out and drained as usual. He sighed, running a hand through his hair, and nodded in my general direction without making eye contact. "Hey," he said, his voice conflicted. I didn't have to ask what it was about. It was Tuesday, which meant we had reached the official start of our arrangement.

Abiding by our rules, Peter hadn't asked me anything about my date or what my plans were, but I could tell it was driving him crazy. I smiled and stood from the chair, walking toward him as he approached the sink to start his evening pot of coffee. "How was work?"

"Fine," he mumbled, either distracted or agitated, but I didn't pry.

"I'm going to go up and get ready. Do you need anything from me first?"

I waited for an answer, which didn't come right away. Instead, he shut the water off, set the half-filled pot down, and turned to face me. "Are you sure about this? Are we sure we know what we're doing? Is this a huge mistake?"

My face warmed from his concern. "I don't think it's a mistake. Do you?"

His brown eyes found mine. "I don't know, Ainsley... I just can't help feeling like after tonight...there's no going back, you know? Up until you walk out that door, we still have a choice, but once it's done...you can't take it back."

I narrowed my gaze at him, taking in what he was

saying. "I hear you," I said, nodding along. "But...what options are there? We both agree it's not working like it is. Marriage counseling and date nights didn't work, so...do we give up? Do we tuck our tails and accept that we have only a few years left of being roommates with the same last name and then pass Maisy her birthday cake as we sign the divorce papers? Even if we decide to stick it out for the kids, do you think we deserve to live like that? Eight years of...what? Some subpar existence?" I drew in my lips. "I don't want to do this, Peter. I'm just as terrified as you are, trust me. I would never have suggested it if I thought we had any other choice, so if you have an option that doesn't involve accepting defeat, I'm all ears." I tucked my hands in my pockets, watching him mull over what I'd said.

"It feels wrong," he said. "I can't explain it. It feels like we're cheating on each other."

"But we aren't. This is an agreement. We're agreeing to see other people to reignite the spark in our marriage. Cheating would involve lying, and there's no lying allowed in this arrangement. I'm with you that it feels strange, but wrong? Wrong would imply that we're doing something shady, and we aren't at all. At least, not to each other."

"You aren't going to fall in love with him, are you?" he asked with a laugh, but I knew he wasn't joking.

I reached out a hand and took his. "This isn't about love. It isn't about sex either. It's about connecting with other people. Having fun. Allowing ourselves to step outside of this mold we've created for our lives and see if there's a part of us that we still need to discover. We used to be whole people without each other and without the kids. I want us to find out what parts of those people still exist. There's nothing that says we have to do anything—physical or otherwise—on these dates. We can talk to people, dance, have a nice dinner, see a movie. I think this is more about connecting with ourselves again than it is about anyone else."

He nodded, but it was slow. Inconsequential. I couldn't tell if he agreed. "You're probably right," he said. "I don't want it to be a mistake."

"There's no mistake we can't fix as long as we work together, okay?" I squeezed his hand before dropping mine to my side. "We're in this together. All the way."

He leaned down, surprising me by kissing my lips. It was the first time he'd done that in I couldn't recall how long. "I love you so much."

"I love you, too." With that, I smiled at him one last time before departing from the room. I needed time to get ready for my first date in over fifteen years.

The date was with a man named Stefan. He was in his mid-forties, so a few years older than Peter and me, bald, with thick, dark eyebrows à la Eugene Levy, and a kind smile. His profile said he liked pasta and wine, he was a proud Italian, and he had a pet Labradoodle named Lip, after Lip Gallagher. He was a widower getting back on the wagon—I guess said wagon came in the form of me tonight—and wanting to have some fun in the process.

We'd talked sporadically over the past few days. He'd sent me a few notes to say *hey* and ask how my days were going, but I'd kept the conversation to a minimum. I wanted to make sure it was clear straight from the get-go that this wasn't a permanent thing, but how would I do that? I should've stuck to matching with twenty-some-things. All they seemed to care about was racking up an astronomical number of women to sleep with. But I'd always been drawn to good conversation over a spectac-ular bedding, and I would assume experienced, older men could bring both to the table.

If I had to guess, I'd bet Peter's date would be younger, maybe much, and brunette. He'd always had a thing for brunettes with hair down to their asses. But, I would play by the rules, and I wouldn't ask him about her or about what they would do together.

A knot formed in my stomach as I forced the thought away. I needed to focus. I needed to get this right. I grabbed the red dress from my closet, a favorite of mine and one I didn't get to wear nearly enough, and laid it out on the bed. It was a midi sleeveless dress with elegant pleats across the chest and a tapered waistband. One of the few silk items of clothing I owned, and certainly the only one I'd ever had dry-cleaned.

I sat down at the vanity, pulling and prodding at my skin. I thought wrinkles were reserved for women in their forties and fifties, but I had discovered my first at age twenty-six, and I'd been on the steady decline ever since. I used to think it was a good thing I managed to snag my husband before my age started to affect my appearance, but now I had to wonder if I'd made a mistake. If things fell apart with Peter and me, the next person wouldn't get me at my best. No one would ever again see what my body looked like before it created and birthed three chil-dren. No one would know how soft and supple my skin was in my early twenties. They wouldn't know who I was when I was carefree and fun. Peter got that version of me, and he'd practically squandered it.

I picked up the bottle of makeup remover, washing away the day. Underneath all the primer, eyeliner, and subtle hints of rouge, I was pale and lifeless. A shell of the woman I once was. I rubbed moisturizer on before adding fresh primer, then put on a new coat of makeup, adding extra color to my cheeks. I dusted gold powder across my eyes—it had always made the green stand out the most—and applied fresh red lipstick, fiery as my hair.

When I was done, I pulled my hair down from its clip and took out the curling wand, turning my flat, red hair into carefree beach waves. It took time, but I still had an hour before I was meeting Stefan and I wanted to look my best.

Once every piece of my hair had been curled to loose, *imperfect* perfection, I spritzed my favorite perfume on my wrists and behind my ears and removed my clothing, slipping on clean, uncomfortable underwear I hadn't worn in years. Next, I unzipped the dress and stepped into it, zipping it back up on the side and adjusting it. Without checking the mirror yet, I made my way into the closet and picked out simple, black heels.

I stood still for a moment, trying to calm my erratic breathing. I shouldn't have felt so afraid. I'd been preparing myself for days, trying to be confident that this would all work out, that Stefan would be great, that Stefan would not be a serial killer, that I would be able to get back into the swing of things easily, that there wouldn't be dating protocol I was unfamiliar with after years of not dating. I wrung my hands together in front of me, sucking in a deep breath and letting it out. My palms were sweaty and I didn't dare wipe them on the silk, so I flapped them at my sides as if I were a bird instead. I could feel sweat beading on my upper lip and along my temple, and I felt both very cold and like I may get sick all at once.

I balled my hands into fists, locking my jaw into a determined grimace. *No.* Tonight would be fun. I was going to make sure it was fun.

I stalked back across the room, pulled out a simple, black clutch, and placed my ID and credit card inside. I looked down at my hand, at the wedding and engagement bands that adorned my ring finger. *Bite the bullet.* I twisted the rings, easing them off my finger and dropping them in the glass ring holder on my vanity. Then, I grabbed my phone and headed for the door. I stopped by the kids' bedrooms one by one.

I reached Dylan's first. He hardly looked up from his tablet, except to mumble "Why are you dressed like that?"

"I have a work thing," I said, the answer I'd prepared. "I won't be home until late. Be good for your dad, okay?"

He nodded, bored with the conversation, and looked back down without another word. I kissed his scruffy brown hair, ruffling it and hurrying from the room before I found myself unable to put off my desire to clean it.

Next came Riley. He was elbow-deep in a bag of potato chips when I walked into the room, one hand on an Xbox controller. He paused it, looking me up and down with a slack jaw and confused expression. "Are we going somewhere?"

"No. Not you, just me. I have a work thing tonight. I probably won't be back before you go to bed. Is your homework done?"

He nodded, appearing relieved. "I only had math, and I finished most of it in class."

"Good. Will you mind your dad for me?"

He rolled his eyes, but unlike Dylan, there was a playfulness there. He'd not yet learned to be annoyed by my every word. "I always do."

"Help him out if he needs it, okay? And don't fight with your brother." I ruffled his hair too, kissing his cheek. He swiped it away with his hand—he didn't used to do that. When did it start? I couldn't even remember.

"I won't. Have fun at your work thing."

"I will," I said. "Love you, kiddo. See you later tonight or in the morning, depending…"

"Love you, too." With that, he pressed the button to start the game back up, and the music began blaring once again. I grabbed a stack of dirty cups from his dresser and walked from the room. I didn't know why I felt so sad about this. It wasn't like I was doing anything to hurt them, but somehow it felt like more of a betrayal to them than it did to Peter.

The last room was Maisy's. The pink flower on her door was one we'd painted together at a Mommy and Me class when she was six, her name drawn out in an attempted fancy script. It was a small sign of what used to be. Her room had changed so much over the years, starting out with posters of rainbows, unicorns, and her favorite Disney princesses, and ending up now with photos of her with her friends, quotes from her favorite books, and string lights all around the top of her walls and hanging in lines behind the head of her bed. I pushed the door open, and she looked up at me from the book in her hand, did a double take, and her brows raised.

"You look *gorg*, Momma. Why are you so dressed up?"

"I've got a meeting with a few people from the office tonight. I'll probably be out late. Think you'll be okay to hang out here with the boys?"

She wrinkled her nose, pretended to think it over, and then nodded. "I think I'll manage."

"What are you reading?" I asked, setting the cups from Riley's room on top of her dresser and easing down on the edge of her bed.

She held up the novel *The Graveyard Book.* "Neil Gaiman." One of her favorite authors. She was a reader, like her father. And like her mother, my sweet Maisy had always been obsessed with all things creepy—ghost stories, scary movies, and the like. I'd been just the same growing up—there wasn't a *Goosebumps* episode or Steven King film I hadn't seen by age thirteen. The ones that existed then, anyway.

"That's a good one," I assured her. "Did you finish your homework?" I didn't even have to ask, but I wanted to. I wanted to savor every moment with her. At that moment, I was hit with the heaviest pang of guilt, and I considered calling the whole thing off to stay home and spend time with her. How long had it been since we'd painted each other's nails and ate junk food together? Did she have a boyfriend? Was there a guy she had a crush on? Once, I would've known that, but I couldn't remember the last time we'd had a real conversation. I missed her.

"Mostly. I have a call with Jennessa and Bailey in an hour to go over our English assignment. It's a group project, but we're going to FaceTime and work on it since Bailey's grounded."

I nodded. So, even if I wanted to stay, I'd be unwelcome. She had plans. Things to do. I would be in the way, and I needed to busy myself. "Anything I can help with?"

"Not really," she said, confirming what I suspected.

"Okay then. Well," I rubbed my hands over my legs, "I'm going to go ahead and get out of here. If you need anything, your dad will be around and I'll have my phone."

"We'll be fine, Mom." She was smiling, and there was no hint of frustration in her tone, but I heard more than what she said nonetheless. They didn't need me anymore. Not like they once had. I felt a tug somewhere deep inside of my stomach, as if the part of me that had grown my children was crying out. I fought back against the bitterness that filled my chest, my jaw tight. My babies were growing up, my husband was growing distant, and my life was at a standstill. The reality of where I was made me ache for all that had been. I touched her cheek lovingly and she looked disturbed, so I let my hand drop.

"Love you, kiddo. Have a good night."

She picked the book back up, already lost in the story. "You too," she called when I pulled open the door and grabbed the stack of cups again.

I made my way down the hall, a hurricane of sadness, confusion over the sadness, anxiety, and fear welling inside of me. I needed to get out of this house before I backed down. Peter was in the kitchen, head in the refrigerator, but when he heard my heels on the hardwood, he looked over his shoulder.

I saw the shock in his eyes. The appreciation for the way I looked.

He was realizing I still had it, though I wouldn't have known it myself if not for that moment. His shocked expression filled me with confidence.

"Y-you look...wow," his gaze bounced from my chest to my eyes and back down again, "you look amazing."

I felt the heat rise to my cheeks, glanced down, and walked past him on my way to place the dirty dishes in the sink. "Thank you."

"He must be taking you somewhere nice."

I froze, processing what he'd said. There was no question in his words at face value, but I knew the intention was there. It was the first hint that he wanted to break the rules. But if I told him anything, he'd want me to tell him everything. We'd be breaking the guidelines we'd laid out. "He is," I said simply, choosing clipped honesty over reiterating the rules.

"Well, he's a...lucky guy tonight."

There was nothing light about his tone then. He was angry. Bitter. I could sense it, but I wouldn't respond. The clock on the stove showed it was after six, which meant I needed to leave the house within the next few minutes to make it to the restaurant by seven.

"Thank you," I said. "I've told the kids I'm heading out, let them know it was a work thing and that I'll see them either late tonight or in the morning. Homework's done, Maisy has a FaceTime thing for one of her assignments here soon, so you won't want to disturb her. Riley needs

27

to eat more than potato chips for dinner, so if you don't cook—"

"I'm going to cook," he affirmed.

"Well, if you don't—"

"I'm going to," he said again, more firmly this time.

"Okay," I nodded. "Fine. Okay. Good." I sighed. "I'll see you when I get home then." I started to walk away, but he stopped me, grabbing my arm.

"Do you—" He let me go when I glanced down at his grip. "Sorry. Do you want to send me his name, or the address of the restaurant, or the name of where you're going in case…I don't know, in case he ends up being some sort of wacko? I know it's against the rules, but…"

I twisted my lips in thought. "I guess it's not the worst idea. How about this: do we have any envelopes?"

"What? Are you going to write me a letter?"

"I'm going to write down his name and the place he's taking me for dinner and seal it in an envelope. Then, when I get home, we can shred it and I'll know if you tampered with it. But if I don't come home or if you don't hear from me, you can open it."

He didn't look happy about the plan. "You don't trust me not to look?"

"It's not about trust. It's about temptation. Knowing you can't look takes away the temptation, and then neither of us has to worry about it."

He sighed. "Fine. Whatever. I'll get an envelope."

I removed a piece of paper from a drawer and scribbled the words down as he sulked out of the room, and when he returned, I slid the paper inside the envelope and sealed it tight. I pulled a piece of tape from the drawer and placed it over the seal. Then, I signed my name to the tape. "There, now it's sealed for sure." It was an old trick we used at the bank to protect the combinations we kept sealed in our keybox from the prying eyes of other employees. The safeguard worked just as well in this situation. If he removed the tape, I'd know it. And he couldn't forge my signature well enough to replace it.

Peter looked at it as if it was the most ridiculous thing in the world, but he didn't say anything.

"Put it on top of the refrigerator so none of the kids find it. I don't want them asking questions."

He did as he was told. "Well, have a good night, I guess."

I nodded, pressing my lips to his cheek awkwardly. "This feels weird," I admitted as I turned away from him.

"So weird," he agreed with a huff of relieved breath.

"I'll text you when I get there. Let you know I made it okay."

"Be careful," he said, the anger disappearing from his eyes, replaced by sadness. "There are a lot of crazy people out there."

"I will be. Promise."

With that, I walked out of the room, then out of the house, refusing to let myself question if I was making the biggest mistake of my life.

CHAPTER FOUR

PETER

I had signed myself up for a specific kind of torture when I brought up the idea of writing down who my wife was currently on a date with. Of course, I hadn't expected her to seal it. I should've, I guess. My wife was nothing if not thorough. Somehow, though, I hadn't seen it coming.

As the evening progressed, I found myself staring at the top of the refrigerator more and more, so much so that Maisy and Riley had both asked me if something was wrong, and even Dylan seemed to have noticed something definitely wasn't right. I'd managed to whip up a quick dinner despite my distraction and carry on a half-hearted conversation throughout the meal, but as soon as it was over and the kids had retired back to their bedrooms, I knew it was going to be a long night of worrying.

I glanced at the doorway to the kitchen again, my throat dry. She texted me around an hour after she left to say that she'd arrived. She was safe. He seemed normal. It was all she'd said. I felt like a girlfriend she'd texted when her date had gone to the bathroom.

I couldn't help wondering what type of man my wife would date. Would she want someone like me? Or someone my opposite? Would she choose someone better looking than me? Someone with better hair? A better build? I couldn't deny that I'd let myself go over the years. Once, I'd had hours a day to spend at the gym, but now, I couldn't remember the last time I'd stepped foot inside one. Things got busy, you know? Between life and work and the kids, there was no time for myself anymore. Not in that way. When you were building an architecture firm from the ground up and raising three children, everything else tended to fall by the wayside. Including my marriage.

Our marriage was good once. I remembered it well. The time when we were inseparable. When all we wanted to do was spend time together. I could've spent hours holding her hand on the couch. We spent entire days at various theaters and restaurants because we had nowhere else to be. And then there were the hours spent rolling around in bed, soaked in sweat, never tiring, never running out of desire for one another. What had become of those people? Why had we let them go?

I felt stupid and selfish for what we were doing. The moments of thrill came, sure, but they were vastly outnumbered by the moments of shame. Shame that I'd let it get to that point. Shame that my wife was looking for happiness in the arms of another man. Shame that my kids had no idea what we were doing or why.

Ainsley was a catch, plain and simple, and I was very worried I'd forgotten that to the point that I might not be able to get her back. To the point that I might lose her. As I thought about it, I made up my mind then and there. When she arrived home that evening, I was going to tell her that agreeing to the arrangement had been a mistake. I was going to tell her I wanted to end it. I wanted to go back to who and what we were before. I didn't care what she did on her date; I just didn't want to do it anymore. The idea of another man looking at her, touching her, kissing her, tasting her... It was enough to drive me insane.

I cleaned up the rest of our dinner in a hurry. I was angry and frustrated and trying to avoid looking at the clock on the wall. When I was done, I got on Facebook, scrolling through my newsfeed with glazed-over eyes. I wasn't paying attention. I couldn't focus on anything but the worry.

I searched for Ainsley's profile, clicking on her albums. There were so many memories there. I looked through them, bitter tears in my eyes. She'd documented everything: us taking the children to the zoo, first days of school, Christmases, birthdays, soccer tournaments with Riley, guitar lessons with Dylan, dance with Maisy. There were photos of the days and early weeks when we'd brought each of them home, the quiet moments we spent just appreciating the little lives we'd brought into the world. Further back, there were a few photos of our wedding. We looked so happy then. I wished I could feel that again. Feel the way I made her eyes light up in the early days. How long had it been since she looked at me that way? I had no idea, and that was painful.

I should've tried harder. Fought for her more.

As I stared at the photos, knowing she was sitting across from another man in a dimly lit restaurant—or, God forbid, that they'd made it even further than that and relocated somewhere more private—I realized I'd given up on her. Not consciously, but somewhere along the line, I had. Why hadn't I made more of an effort to make sure the date nights she so desperately desired happened? Why hadn't I been more open and honest in couples counseling? Why had I cancelled more sessions than I'd attended? She'd fought so hard for us, making suggestion after suggestion, and I'd just let them all fall through the cracks. I'd never put in any effort. Was I too late now?

I was so angry with myself.

So furious.

I picked up my phone. I wanted to stop her before things got out of hand. There was still time. I selected her name from my contacts and listened to it ringing.

Please pick up. Please pick up. Please pick up.

After three rings, I was sent to voicemail. She'd ignored the call. Panic swelled in me, traveling from the knot in my stomach to a newly forming balloon in my chest. I looked back at the doorway to the kitchen. My chance to fix this was in there. My chance to fight for her before we took this step. Before she slept with him. Would she be furious with me for breaking the rules? Chances were, absolutely. But I didn't care. I didn't want her to be with him. I didn't want anyone else to have the opportunity to make her happy.

I reached the refrigerator and grabbed the envelope from the top. The envelope was dusty, and I made a mental note to clean the top of the refrigerator for her once everything had blown over.

Without allowing myself to think about it too much, I tore open the envelope, making no effort to hide the evidence. I pulled the note out and unfolded it. Her scrawled handwriting could be seen through the paper.

I turned it over, reading with disbelief what she'd written.

No.

I read it again, shaking my head.

> **Sorry, honey.**
> **Rules are rules.**

I checked both sides, looking over it for more. I should've known she wouldn't trust me not to check. I groaned, slamming my hand onto the counter, the note crumpled in my palm.

What had I done?

IT WAS JUST after one in the morning when she arrived home. I was asleep on the couch when she came through the door. I jolted, taking a good look at her, ice-cold dread ricocheting through me. Her lipstick was gone, but that could've been from eating and drinking. Her hair looked the same, her clothing was not rumpled or disheveled.

I let out a sigh of relief, thankful that she was safe. That she'd come back to me. But I couldn't deny the innate curiosity roaring through me.

When I sat up, she smiled at me, ducking her head a little bit. I had so much I wanted to say, so much I'd saved up, but at that moment, no words would come. I couldn't bring myself to give her the speech I'd prepared, not when she looked so unbelievably happy.

"How did it go?" she asked, keeping her distance from me.

"Everything was fine here," I squeaked out. My body shook from all I was trying to conceal—the anger over the note, the fury at myself for letting her leave, the relief that she was home, the worry about what she'd done. My mind raced with possibilities and endless questions, each fighting to be heard and answered.

"Are the kids asleep?"

I nodded, my lips pressed together as if I were physically holding in the inquisition I wanted to unleash.

"Okay, well...I'm going to go take a shower, then." A small, sly smile played on her lips again, causing bile to rise in my throat. What was she showering off? Better yet, *who* was she showering off? I knew then that she'd slept with him. That it had been done. She'd betrayed me in the worst way.

I knew it wasn't betrayal. I understood it was agreed upon. But that didn't make it any less painful. Permission to break my heart didn't make the ache any less devastating. I don't think I ever responded, though she walked away. She made her way down the hall, and I could hear her humming as she went.

I headed that direction, with no real plan for what I'd do once I reached her. When I got to the door, though, I chickened out. There was nothing left to say. Instead, I returned to our bedroom and crawled into bed. The tears found me there, and I let them fall until I heard her open our bedroom door.

She came straight from the bathroom to the bedroom, wrapped in a towel. She dressed in the dark, as if there might be evidence of what she'd done on her body. Maybe there was. I squeezed my eyes shut, refusing to look at her. She probably believed I was asleep, and I made no move to correct her.

She didn't check the refrigerator, not when she arrived home and not before she climbed into bed with me, our bodies inches apart. I don't think she needed to. She knew me too well. She'd always said she knew me better than I knew myself. Which meant she knew I'd opened it; it was why she wrote what she did.

It seemed as if my wife knew my every move before I even made it, but I could've never guessed her moves that night.

I never thought she'd go through with it. That was the bitter truth. I thought she'd change her mind. I thought she loved me too much.

But she didn't.

She'd gone through with it. She'd slept with someone else.

And that changed everything.

CHAPTER FIVE

AINSLEY

I could hardly sleep. I tossed and turned, waking and readjusting over and over, and when I woke up the final time a few hours later, Peter and I didn't talk about what happened.

He didn't ask any questions, though I knew he wanted to. There were a few times when he stopped, standing in the middle of our bedroom as we both got ready for the day, and stared at me. His mouth would hang open as if he was trying to coax the question from his depths.

Each time though, without a word, he'd end up walking away. He didn't ask what I did or how it went... he didn't ask anything, but it was there in his face. The questions. The burning desire to know everything. It made it more exciting in a way. Peter and I had been together for so many years, sometimes it felt as if we no longer had secrets. Until that moment.

Finally, we both knew we had secrets again, and we'd only be creating more. I smiled to myself as I slid the maroon lipstick over my lips. He was watching me again, but I pretended not to notice. The truth was much less exciting than whatever he'd cooked up in his head. Maybe that was why the process would work—if it did, *when* it did. Because all he'd be able to think about for the next several days, weeks maybe, was me with someone else. Someone else doing his job, someone else loving me like he should have. Perhaps the jealousy would give him motivation to improve.

"I've got an early morning," he said, breaking the silence. It was the first sentence either of us had spoken since our alarms had gone off at five that morning. "Can you get the kids to school?"

"Mhm," I said, not nodding as I continued to glide the lipstick across my lips, making sure the lines were razor sharp.

He took a step toward me, and I lowered the tube, placing the lid back on it and meeting his eye in the mirror. To my surprise, he placed a hand on the side of my head, leaning down and pressing his lips to my temple. "Have a good day," he whispered before standing back up.

"You too," I said, turning around to look at him. "I'll see you tonight."

He nodded but didn't look back as he crossed the room and opened the door. Within seconds, he had disappeared and I was left alone with my thoughts, which I'd been trying to quiet.

The truth was, my date with Stefan went fine. He was nice, polite. He paid for my meal and drinks, asked about my career, told me about his. We talked about dating after a long-term relationship, and he only mentioned his late wife once. He held my hand as he walked me to my car. Everything was there. Everything was perfect.

But I didn't go home with him. He didn't ask me to, but I knew he would've taken me up on it if I'd mentioned it. I'd watched his gaze trail down the length of my dress or the stretch of my exposed cleavage when he thought I wasn't looking. He wasn't a pig about it, don't get me wrong. But he was a man who hadn't been with a woman in a very long time, and that was clear.

So why didn't I go home with him? He was attractive, sweet, interested... But the truth was, I couldn't turn off the guilt I felt. Not about Peter. We'd agreed to this. He wasn't going to feel guilty about it when it was his turn. Instead, my guilt manifested about Stefan. I knew my night with him would be just the one. I didn't plan to see him ever again. Our date hadn't meant anything to me. It was purely to meet a need.

Perhaps I read him wrong and that was all he wanted too, but from the questions he asked about my life, the things he shared about himself, I got the impression that he was truly trying to get to know me. He mentioned more than once that I was the first woman he'd taken on a date in a long time, only one of those times specifying since his wife had passed away. It felt huge. It felt like I was stringing him along. I didn't want to be the first woman he slept with after his wife died and then break his heart by never contacting him again. It felt wrong. And as much as this process was supposed to be about healing Peter and me, I felt awful that Stefan had gotten caught in the crossfire.

Once my makeup was finished, I spritzed my face with

setting spray, ran my flat iron over my hair a few strokes more, and pulled on my black slacks and blouse with a pearl necklace to top off the outfit. I stepped into my favorite nude heels and headed for the door. The kids were bustling around the house, and Dylan crossed in front of me, dressed in only his boxers.

"Have you seen my green hoodie?"

"Good morning, Mom. How are you?" I asked sarcastically.

"This is serious!" he said. I was starting to think irritation was the only tone he knew. "I can't find it anywhere. Riley's been taking my stuff!"

"I have not!" The faint argument came from beyond the closed door in the bedroom to our left. Riley swung open his bedroom door, completely dressed, with half of a Pop-Tart in his hand. "Mom, I didn't touch his stuff!"

"When did you have it last?" I asked Dylan.

"Friday at school, but I brought it home to be washed, and I never got it back."

"Did you check the laundry room? Maybe it's in the dryer."

"It's not, I checked!" he grumbled, casting an angry look at his brother. "Riley keeps coming into my room and taking my stuff. That hoodie is my favorite. I have to find it."

"I haven't touched your—"

"Okay, boys," I cut off the impending argument. "We don't have time for this. I'm sorry, Dylan, but you'll have to wear a different hoodie today. I'll find it this afternoon, okay? We have to get going, or we're all going to be late."

"Ugh, *Mom,* I can't go to school without it!"

"Well, that's a problem because you're going to have to," I said, walking away from the argument before anything else could be said. "Come on. We have ten minutes."

The boys groaned but separated back toward their rooms as Maisy appeared in the hallway, dressed and ready to go. She had two library books and three school books in her arms. "Morning."

"Morning, sweetheart. How did last night go? Did you finish your project?"

She nodded. "Yep, all done. How was your work thing?"

"It was fine," I told her simply. "Have you had breakfast?"

"Oatmeal. Where's Dad?"

"Oh, he had to get to work early." She twisted her mouth in deep thought, and it occurred to me then: did the children know something was up? Did they suspect that Peter and I were avoiding each other? Had we done a terrible job acting like things were still normal? Tonight would be a good time to prove them wrong, all of us together as a family. "Did you need something from him?"

"Huh? Oh, no. Nothing. I hadn't seen him this morning."

"He wanted to say goodbye, but I think we're all running a bit behind." I was always making excuses for him, I realized. Like it was ingrained in me. Not that Peter was an absentee father. He was far from it, in fact. He came home on time, rarely worked overtime, and was with us during the weekend. He was as involved as I was, and yet I felt the need to overcompensate and explain away the few failings he had. Why was that? What had he done to warrant my intense worry that the kids would see him as less than perfect? Did he do the same for me? I doubted it.

"Okay, well, I'm going to make my tea before I head to the car. Do you want anything?"

She shook her head. "I'll meet you in the garage."

As I made my way into the kitchen and put the kettle on for my morning tea, I heard the boys coming out of their rooms. I turned around, surprised to see Dylan wearing the green hoodie he'd been looking for.

"You found it, then?"

"It was hanging up by the door," he mumbled, opening the cabinet and pulling out a small bag of Doritos. I'd argue it wasn't a good breakfast, but I didn't have the energy. Instead, I watched him shove it in the front pocket of his hoodie as he stalked out of the room. Within a few minutes, my tea kettle began to squeal, and I placed an English Breakfast Tea bag into my travel mug and poured the hot water into it, sealing the lid and grabbing a protein bar from the cabinet above the refrigerator. As I did it, I remembered the note. It was on my mind when I came home last night, but I didn't dare check it in front of Peter. I didn't want him to know I'd been expecting him to open it. I pulled the white envelope down, not surprised but definitely disappointed to realize I was right. The envelope had been torn open; he'd made no effort to seal it back or hide the evidence.

I ripped it in half and tossed it into the trash can, wondering how he must've felt when he saw what I'd written.

I sipped the tea, hardly aware of it scalding my mouth as I rushed out of the house. Though I wanted to unpack why my husband hadn't trusted me, why he'd broken the rules so early into our arrangement, I had to get the kids to school and myself to work before we were all late.

Life wasn't going to slow down because of our crisis.

I just had to learn to keep up.

CHAPTER SIX

PETER

I t felt like getting family portraits, that moment when the photographer tells you to stand still and smile, and all you can think of is: *where do I put my hands? Why am I so aware of my breathing? Does this smile look forced?*

That was the only way I could think of to explain the way I felt. The way I'd felt from the moment Ainsley made it home from her date. Sleep didn't make it any better. I tossed and turned all night, waking for the final time two hours before my alarm was set to go off and deciding to get up anyway.

I didn't know what to say around her, how to act, what to do. Multiple times, I caught myself staring at her in a strange, trance-like state with no idea what I was thinking. It was as if I couldn't look away. As if she were a celebrity or a car crash, pulling my eyes to her with every move that she made.

There was such mystery to her now. What had she done? What had she said? What had she told him about our lives? Had she liked him? Had she kissed him? Had

44

she done much, much more? So many questions haunted me, begging to be answered. I couldn't bring myself to move on, but I was not allowed to ask anything.

Was this how she would feel when it was my turn? I didn't want to think about it. I was embarrassed by all of it. Since I'd matched with Gina, we hadn't spoken to each other, passing in the halls without a word. Perhaps she was doing it as a test. Perhaps she matched with me as an accident and my matching back with her made it awkward and confusing, as neither of us seemed to know how to approach the subject. I should've never done anything so stupid. I felt weak and angry with myself for my lack of control. Why couldn't I stop myself from acting so impulsively?

I sat at my desk that afternoon, staring at the screen filled with numbers and words that my eyes continued to glaze over. I read emails and memos over and over, unable to form clear, coherent thoughts. I couldn't seem to focus on anything else. I picked up the paper cup of coffee, sipping it as I wondered how we'd gotten so off course. Why had I ever agreed to this? Why hadn't I told her no when she suggested it?

The door to my office opened, and I looked up, hating the hope and worry that filled my chest all at once when I saw her.

"Gina, hey," I said, standing from my desk like the idiot I was.

She smiled, but it seemed forced. Stiff. "Hey, Peter... Sorry, I was wondering if you'd finalized your portion of the report for the Gregory project yet. They're starting to get impatient."

"Shoot." I put my fingers to my forehead and sank into my chair. "I thought I'd sent it back to you already." I scrolled through my email, cursing under my breath. "Dammit," I said when my eyes landed on the draft in my outbox, sitting unsent for almost a week. "Here it is." I pressed send and groaned. "I'm so sorry. I thought I'd sent it Monday afternoon. I've been distracted, I guess..."

She nodded but didn't say anything right away. She waited to see if I'd say more before going on. "I need to tell you something," she said hesitantly. I watched as her eyes rolled, my throat dry. Was she going to tell me it was all a prank or a joke and she was feeling awkward about it? Was she going to tell me she was quitting because I'd made things too weird between us?

I turned my chair toward her, resting my hands in my lap. "Okay. What's up?"

"I think someone may be using your pictures to catfish people."

I sucked in a breath. Whatever I'd been expecting her to say, that wasn't it. She may as well have been speaking a foreign language. "*Catfish* someone? What are you talking about? What pictures?"

She rolled her eyes again and sat down in one of the chairs in front of my desk, her cheeks flushed pink. "Okay, well, it's kind of embarrassing to admit, but I do a fair bit of online dating." She paused, as if she thought I might say something or laugh, but I remained quiet and waited. She went on. "And, well, the other day, I saw someone using your pictures under the name Pete Patterson." She pulled out her phone and scrolled through it while I sat, contemplating my next move. I could've gone along with it, pretended that the person wasn't me, or I could've told the truth. I had no idea which one was the best course of action. She held out her phone to me, where I could look over *Pete's* profile. "We matched because I was planning on calling him out for using the pictures, but then I wondered, well…it's stupid. You're happily married. Of course you aren't on a dating site. I'm planning to report him." Her last few sentences came out at lightning speed as her face grew a deeper shade of scarlet. "I wanted to tell you, so you didn't think… I don't know. I guess I'd want to know if it were me." She sucked her teeth, looking away. "Anyway…" She slapped her legs, moving to stand. "You sent that over to me, you said, right? Yes."

"Gina, wait," I called as she moved toward the door, something deep in my stomach lurching as she grew farther away. "Wait."

She looked over her shoulder then spun further around, one brow raised with an unspoken question.

I had no idea what I was going to say until the words were leaving my mouth. "I'm embarrassed. I don't know what to say. Ainsley and I are…spending some time apart. We agreed on seeing other people. When I saw you on the app, I knew it was stupid to match with you, but…I acted on a whim. I'm sorry if it's made things awkward for you."

Her eyes lit up, her lips separating slightly as she stared at me. "Wait, so you're saying… You *are* Pete Patterson? It really *is* you?"

I laughed, nodding my head. "It's embarrassing. The fake names were Ainsley's idea, to keep some privacy in the situation and protect our kids. We don't want them finding out what's going on until things are official…one way or another."

She was slow to nod, studying me as she moved a half-step forward. There was a glint of fascination in her eyes. "No, no, I understand. Of course. I'm sorry I brought it up. Maybe you'd rather I hadn't?"

"No, not at all. It's not your fault. I'm glad you did. I guess we never thought about seeing someone we knew from *real life* on the app. The plan was to keep it so anyone we dated couldn't find us. When I saw you there, it took me by surprise."

Her lips widened as she appeared to think, giving way to the perfect, white teeth behind them. "But you matched with me on purpose?"

"Stupidly, maybe, but yes. I'm still new to all of this…" I trailed off, feeling the heat rushing to my face. "And I know it makes things awkward because we work together, so if you think we should pretend it never happened, we can totally do that."

"Is that what you want?" I gulped, embarrassed by the sudden noise, but she didn't flinch. "Because I'm okay with that if you are. I don't want to get in the middle of anything…" She waved her hand in a circular direction, as if she were a witch stirring a cauldron.

"No, you wouldn't. I mean, I don't want or need anything complicated right now. I'm trying out the online dating thing to…"

"To have a little fun?" she asked, her tongue pressed to her teeth as she cocked her head to the side.

"Mhm," I said, barely making an audible noise in the deafening silence. She waited. I cleared my throat and pressed my hands together in front of my chest. "That probably sounds lame."

She laughed. "Now *that* sounded *lame.*" She said *lame* as if it were an uncool word, and I realized then the stark age gap between us. "Tell you what, you think about what you want for sure, and when you know... Have *Pete Patterson* send me a message. Otherwise, I'll see *you, Peter,* later. Thanks for the report." I nodded, but she didn't see it. Her hand was already on the door handle as she prepared to leave.

"Gina?" I called, half standing from my chair.

She looked over her shoulder, her brows raised. "Yeah?"

"It probably goes without saying, but I wanted to ask for your discretion with all of this. I try to keep my personal life separate from the office as much as possible, and I'd appreciate it if you kept what I've told you between us."

"Of course, Peter. You don't even have to ask. It'll be our little secret." She winked at me and pulled the door open, sauntering out of my office without another word.

My body tingled with the possibilities and adrenaline from the conversation. *What the hell just happened?*

My phone lay facedown on the desk, taunting me, but I couldn't act yet. I had to think rationally, and the overwhelming excitement I was feeling wasn't rational at all.

CHAPTER SEVEN

AINSLEY

Stefan had sent me two messages since the night before. One after I got home to say how much fun he had with me and another that morning to say though he knew he should've waited to ask, he'd like to see me again if I'd be open to it.

I hadn't responded to either message.

How could I?

I hadn't come to grips with my feelings over everything. Originally, my goal was to fix my marriage, to make my husband realize what he was risking losing. But I didn't want to have to hurt anyone in the process, especially a decent, caring man like Stefan. It wasn't his fault we'd connected. It wasn't his fault my only goal was to reconnect with the husband I was losing.

I didn't want him to get hurt in the process of me trying to clean up my mess of a marriage, and that was what was happening. He was interested in me, and I'd purposefully chosen a man who seemed caring. A man who would make me feel listened to.

This was all my fault. I hadn't expected the guilt to weigh on me so heavily.

At the end of business, after the branch had closed and the tellers had balanced out their cash drawers, I closed the door to my office, locking it up and making my way toward the alarm console. "You guys ready?"

"Yep," came the reply. The tellers, Tara and Brendan, walked around from behind the counter and hurried toward the door, laughing about some joke I wasn't privy to. I'd worked my way up from their position as a teller myself, to a lead banker, and three years ago, I'd become the branch manager. The moment the change took place, I found myself no longer allowed to join in on the laughter. No longer *invited* in. I'd become the boss, which apparently meant I was to be feared, not welcomed into the closest circles. They were nice enough to me, sure, but I couldn't help noticing, despite having worked with most of them for years, that the moment I took the position, suddenly conversations stopped when I walked into the room. Laughter faded. I became the figure of authority, and no longer was I considered a friend.

I hated it. I missed the laughter. I missed getting to come into work and relax with a coworker between customers. But my ambition had separated me from those I knew and turned me into someone else. At least, that's how it seemed in their eyes. I still felt like myself. The version of myself that needed friends more than ever.

I typed in my code and jogged across the spacious lobby, waiting as Brendan locked the door behind me and the three of us departed the building together. "Have a good night, you two."

"You too. See you tomorrow," Tara called, waving her hand over her head. I let out a heavy breath as I sank into the car. There were days, not so long ago, when I'd rush out of work to pick up the kids from daycare or after-school care. Now, though, they were all so busy with their after-school programs, sports, and friends, I had nowhere to rush to.

So, I sat. And I thought. Which was most often a dangerous thing. I thought about Stefan, whose messages sat unopened on my phone. I thought about Peter, who had never looked at me the way he looked at me that morning. At least he *was* looking at me again, I reasoned, but not in a way that made me proud.

My phone buzzed, and I looked down at it. **Unknown caller.**

It was the second blocked phone call I'd received that day. It wasn't all that unusual for me to receive spam calls, but still, it bothered me. I pressed the button to ignore the call, dropping the phone back into my cup holder.

I had no need to feel guilty for what I'd done—*or hadn't done*, more like. We made an agreement, and my date's steam-level was grade school at best. I didn't cross the lines we'd made way for me to cross, so what was the nagging feeling in my chest I couldn't seem to shake? Why did I feel like I'd ruined something? My marriage? There was no way it could be ruined beyond the point that it already was. My children? Oblivious to what we were doing. My team at work had no idea what I'd been up to. So what was the feeling eating away at me? *Shame.* I sat with the feeling long enough to recognize it, though it didn't belong there. It didn't apply to me. I had no reason to feel ashamed. Not yet.

I wondered who Peter had been talking to, who he'd chosen to take on his first date the next evening. For some strange reason, the feeling didn't make me sick. There was no jealousy in my wonderment. In fact, I felt more bitter that he hadn't been jealous of my date than about my own lack of feelings for him.

Once I was bored with the thinking and feeling, I pulled my car out of the parking spot and out of the lot and headed for home. It felt like I was watching my life unfold before me, rather than living it myself. Was this what a midlife crisis felt like? I didn't feel nearly old enough for a midlife crisis, but that was what the ache seemed to be. The indescribable ache of watching my life pass me by and realizing the best years were behind me. Once, there had been things I looked forward to: birthdays, holidays, vacations. As I'd gotten older, the birthdays came and went with less celebration, the kids preferred cash to gifts on holidays, and they'd rather us order out than spend time cooking a meal together. Though we'd always made it a point to take two week-long vacations a year, the kids were much less interested in doing the dorky family things that we used to enjoy so much— burying Peter in the sand, taking pictures in the shark's mouth at Sharky's, searching for sand dollars together, buying oversized cups from Pineapple Willy's, and building sand castles. Instead, Dylan and Riley now preferred to run headfirst into the ocean and spend their time testing the limits of how far out they could make it. Maisy, our reader, would don a hat and sunglasses and spend her time with her nose in a book, while trying not to get sunburned. We were no longer the family we'd once been, and I wasn't sure when that happened.

I supposed that was what had made me so afraid. I didn't know when my life had become what it was. It all felt like I'd woken up one morning and looked around at my half-grown children, my stagnant career, and a husband who wanted nothing to do with me, and I realized I had no idea how we'd gotten here.

Twenty mind-numbing minutes later, I pulled into our long, gravel driveway. The house was surrounded by acres of forest, miles away from town. We'd longed for privacy and nature when we'd decided to buy our first house, having both grown up in the city with very little yard to play in. As an added bonus, Peter had designed the house himself when we'd found the perfect plot of land. It was his first project after graduation. Though we couldn't afford much at the time, it was cute enough and had been a wonderful home to start and grow our family in. The house was pale brick with red shutters. There was a swing set in the side yard that hadn't been played on in years and a sandbox next to it that was more grass than sand these days. Inside the garage were five bicycles, most of which had flat tires and cracking seats. The reminders were everywhere—things were changing. They'd never be the same. I pulled down the mirror and looked over my face, brushing the tears from my cheeks. I didn't have time to fall apart. Not right then.

When I walked inside, the house was quiet. There were no happy footsteps rushing to greet me, to show me their latest masterpieces or tell me about their days. There were days when they were young when I begged for a minute of peace, a minute to breathe, or shower, or think...but this was worse. Back then, I had no idea how much peace I'd have one day all too soon.

I hung my purse on the coat rack in the hall, removed my peacoat, scarf, and shoes, and headed for the bedroom to change clothes. Once I was comfortable in my pajamas, I headed for the kitchen, where I grabbed the chicken for dinner and the wine for my nerves. I poured a glass and took a sip, the calm flowing through me in an instant.

As I took another sip and reached for a baking dish to start dinner, I heard the hall door from the garage open and Peter's footsteps coming up the stairs. He headed toward the bedroom as I set down the glass of wine and prepared the chicken. I was sliding it into the oven when he appeared behind me, his heavy footsteps a warning he was coming.

"Have a good day?" he asked—all in one breath. His voice was abrupt, as if he'd been rehearsing the question and it spilled out before he was ready.

I closed the oven door and looked over my shoulder. "It was all right. How was yours?"

"Fine," he said. "Listen, I—"

"I wanted—" I said, stopping as we interrupted each other. "You go."

He smiled, shaking his head. "No, you first."

"I wanted to add a new rule to our existing rules," I told him, resting my back against the counter as I lifted the wine glass and spun it in my hand.

"A new rule?" His face fell.

"Nothing crazy. A clarification, I guess. It was pretty

unspoken before, but I want to make it official. I think we should let the people we're seeing know up front that it's a physical, casual thing." His brow inched up a hair, it was barely noticeable, but I noticed. So, I went on. "I just think that's going to be the easiest way to prevent anyone, on either side, from developing feelings. I don't want anyone to get hurt. Don't you agree?"

He opened his mouth wide, like he'd been planning to argue or say something profound, but dropped it back closed. "Yeah," he said eventually. "Yeah, that's fine."

"You seem like you disagree."

He shook his head. "No, it's not that, it's just that... well, I think that'll come off much better from your end than mine. Women are going to think I'm an asshole."

"Trust me, there are as many women out there looking for something casual as there are men—I'm proof of that. We have to be sure we find the right ones. The last thing either of us needs is some needy, scorned one-night stand snooping around." I lowered my voice as I finished the sentence.

He nodded. "Okay. Yeah, that works for me."

"Good." I tapped the metal of my wedding ring against the glass in my hand. "Okay, I'm glad we're on the same page."

"So, did something happen to make you decide this? Are you having trouble with the guy you saw last night?"

"No," I assured him. "It's something I've been thinking about. I had a few messages from him after, and I thought maybe I should've been clearer, so I wanted to give you a heads-up for tomorrow night and going forward."

He nodded. "Okay."

"Speaking of, have you decided who you're going to ask?"

A scowl formed on his face, the crease in his forehead deepening. "It's not the spring formal, Ainsley."

"You know what I mean." I smiled, trying to tamp down the jealousy I was starting to feel dancing in my belly.

"I've decided, yeah."

Who was she? Someone younger? Thinner? Prettier? Someone who wouldn't nag him about anything? I shivered, shunning the thought away. It didn't matter who she was. What mattered was what the process did to my husband, and if his date went anything like mine, there was a chance it could work.

I changed the subject. "Any requests for what to make with the chicken?"

"I was thinking Brussels sprouts," he said, walking toward the refrigerator. "We have some from the produce delivery that need to be cooked before they go bad." He pulled the green bag from the crisper drawer and moved toward the sink to begin washing the vegetables.

"What are you doing?" I asked, because it had been so long since he'd offered me any help with dinner I legitimately couldn't remember the last time it happened.

"I thought I'd help..." His voice was soft and unsure, as if he thought I might scold him for helping me out. "If that's okay?"

"Sure." I took another sip of my wine. "Do you want something to drink?"

"I'm okay," he said, holding my eye contact for an extra second. There was something warm in his eyes that I'd missed. He was trying to impress me, and I couldn't help cherishing that. When he moved to my side to chop and season the vegetables, his hip rested against my side. Though there was plenty of counter space on either side of us, neither of us moved.

I listened to the steady chopping, my body heating up as his skin continued grazing mine, and smiled to myself. Maybe my plan would work out after all.

CHAPTER EIGHT

PETER

When Thursday night rolled around, I was a ball of nerves. The last time I could remember feeling that way was the night Maisy was born. Nervous, excited, worried. I was afraid I'd make a mess of the date, that I'd do something to embarrass myself. Worse, I was afraid I'd do something to inadvertently ruin my marriage. I knew what the rules were, but that didn't stop me from worrying they'd change or I'd somehow break one.

When Ainsley told me the new rule the night before, I wanted so badly to tell her I wanted to call the whole thing off instead. I bounced back and forth between being excited about the possibility of what we were doing, terrified that this would ruin our marriage, ruin our family, and disgusted with the fact that I couldn't let myself enjoy it. What kind of man asks questions when his wife says she wants him to sleep with other people? I couldn't bring myself to tell the nagging voice, the one warning how close I was to losing her, to shut up.

When I was a kid, my parents made me take piano lessons. I painstakingly memorized the notes, memorized where my fingers were supposed to lay on the keys. I remembered the way my piano teacher smelled—like a musty attic and the peppermints she kept in her pockets all rolled into one—and the way she'd rap my knuckles with her ruler whenever my hands lost their posture.

That was how I felt at that moment. Like my life had fallen out of posture and I was waiting for Mrs. Feffermen to smack my knuckles and get me back into shape.

I walked from the bedroom, dressed in dark gray slacks with a light blue button-down shirt and a black bomber jacket. I was nervous as hell when I appeared in the living room—Ainsley apparently oblivious to me for a few seconds as she shredded the baked chicken for her legendary white chicken chili. She moved the metal claws through the meat with precision. Anger. Was I imagining that?

I cleared my throat, and she glanced over her shoulder, then released the claws, grabbing a towel to dry her hands as she looked me over. "You look nice, babe," she said. Her tone was casual. Unbothered. As if I were headed to the grocery store rather than on a date.

I swallowed and stepped forward. "Does the jacket look..." I adjusted it, pulling on the neck. "Is it too much?"

She walked toward me, checking that her hands were clean before she laid the towel down on the counter and reached for the collar, adjusting it. "Are you comfortable?" My wife preferred deep shades of red lipstick, colors that matched her hair. She applied them every morning, and by the evening, they'd all but faded from her lips. I could see traces of her lipstick then, near the edges of her smile and in the cracks of her bottom lip. I was struck by the sudden urge to lean down, take her lip between my teeth, and bite down. I couldn't explain it, the sudden urge to hurt her, but it was there. I wanted to cause her pain. Was that my way of coping?

"I'm comfortable," I said, forcing the thought away. "I haven't worn this jacket enough. It's still stiff."

She ran her hands slowly down my sides, almost sensually, but there was nothing sensual in her eyes. She was slow, methodical, as if I were one of the children trying on an outfit in the dressing room at the mall. She carefully looked over my body in the clothes meant to impress another woman, her lips pressed together. "Well, what if you wore a sweater instead? If you aren't comfortable, it's going to show."

"I don't want to look like a bum."

She scoffed. "You aren't going to look like a bum. You look handsome in sweaters. You always have. You can wear the cashmere one your parents got you last Christmas."

"I'd forgotten about that one," I said. "I mean, I think this looks okay though, right?"

Her eyes bounced up to mine, and I couldn't tell if there was any frustration in them. When we first moved in together, Ainsley used to complain that I was the only man she knew who required several clothing changes before we could leave the house. I liked to try things on, see how they felt against my skin, see how they looked. Did that make me so different from every other man? I didn't know, but it was how I worked.

"You look great," she repeated. "Don't be nervous. Do you have everything you need?"

I nodded, patting my back pocket, where my wallet rested. There was a condom tucked inside, hidden away like I'd done in my teenage years. Was it presumptuous to pack one? I wanted to be prepared, just in case. The thought shot through me like lightning: *I might be having sex tonight. I might be having sex with someone who isn't my wife.*

Why did I feel so excited and terrified all at once? It was enough to make me sick. What if I didn't know what I was doing? I'd only cared about impressing Ainsley for so long, what if I hadn't been kept up to date on what was in anymore? What if there was some new move I didn't know about? What if sex had changed somehow? What if *my* sex had changed? What if I'd gotten lazy? What if I wasn't as good as she pretended I was?

I shuddered, forcing the thought away as she interrupted it by kissing my cheek gently, then rubbing her thumb over where the kiss had landed. "Go on, now. Have fun. What time are you supposed to be there? Are you picking her up?"

I shook my head, clearing my throat. "We're meeting at seven."

We glanced at the clock in unison. It was just after six, so I had plenty of time, but I needed to leave. I needed to get out of her presence, away from her warm, familiar, musky jasmine scent that enveloped the house, and into the groove of things. *Groove of things?* I cringed—even my thoughts were old and uncool. I was a dad, and it was painfully obvious. I needed to get out of my own head.

"Okay, I'll be back later," I said. She didn't ask me to write down the name of the girl or the restaurant. She didn't ask any more questions. Instead, she nodded, turning back to the chicken on the counter and setting to work.

"We'll see you then."

I walked away, out of the room and through the door. She never asked me about the note she'd written and sealed, but I suspected she didn't need to. My wife knew me too well. She knew every thought before I had it, every move before I made it. Strangely, I found comfort in that, knowing that I didn't have to be anyone I wasn't with her. Knowing that my being someone different would surprise her, maybe even disappoint her.

There was uncertainty in the night, the date—spending an evening with someone who didn't know me at all. It was part of the reason I hadn't decided to take Gina up on her offer. It felt wrong somehow. Not that I'd expected her to fall madly in love with me, but I supposed I had too much respect for her to ask her out on a date where: a) I would probably be pretty rusty and awkward, and b) I planned to have sex—if my date was up for it—and never call her again.

So, for my first date, I'd chosen Mallory, a blonde massage therapist in her mid-twenties who loved to watch Hallmark Christmas movies year round and hike with her Shih Tzu, Bebe. Most of her pictures on the app were of her in bikinis, and the rest were either outdoors in tiny shorts or indoors in low-cut pajamas. Maybe it made me shallow to have picked her, but I needed someone who screamed *casual* for my first attempt at dating in years, and that was Mallory to the T.

When I arrived at the restaurant, I was seated in the oversized booth in the far corner. I ordered a gin and tonic for myself and waited. If I were with Ainsley, I'd have ordered her a red wine, a pinot or a cabernet perhaps. I considered guessing for Mallory—I'd bet she was a cosmo girl, but I wasn't sure what the protocol was anymore, and I didn't want to come across as a date rapist. So, instead, I sipped my drink, using my black straw to stir around the slices of lime.

When Mallory arrived, led to the table by a maître d', I stood up, though it was awkward in the booth, and scooted toward the edge, reaching out my hand as she went in for a hug. She was wearing a small, pink dress, with minimal makeup except for giant, fake eyelashes and painted brows. Her blonde hair was cut into a sleek bob, unlike the wild, long hair in her pictures, and she'd straightened the curls I was so fond of.

"It's nice to meet you," she said, her voice deeper than I imagined. She was insanely beautiful, there was no doubt, but everything about her was different than I'd expected. She was calmer, like a dimmer version of the life-of-the-party girl I'd met on the app.

"You too," I said, returning to my seat. "Sorry I didn't order you a drink yet. I wasn't sure what you prefer."

"No worries," she said, waving her hand at me. The waiter reappeared, and she ordered a whiskey neat, making me grateful I hadn't tried to guess her drink, because, given a thousand guesses, that would've never been one of them. She played with a strand of her hair, checking her phone once before sliding it into her purse and watching for the waiter. When he appeared, he placed her drink in front of her and took our orders. For the first time, she didn't surprise me, ordering a small salad while I ordered a burger and fries. A salad was not a meal, something Ainsley and I agreed on, but I didn't bother saying it to her. Who cared if she only ate salads? I'd never see her again after tonight. I had Ainsley to go home to… Ainsley who ate real meals and didn't mind a bit of meat on her bones.

I squeezed my eyes shut, forcing myself to stop thinking of my wife. I was never going to get anywhere on this date if I couldn't stop thinking of her. And, as Mallory leaned into the table, her breasts pressing against the edge and nearly bulging out of the top of her dress, I realized how badly I did want to get somewhere with her. It was almost incessant. I needed to. To prove something —to myself, to my wife. I wanted to feel wanted again. I wanted someone to look at me the way Mallory was looking at me now. I wanted that look to last all night. Why had I allowed myself to forget how good that felt?

"So, tell me about yourself," she said, breaking the silence I hadn't realized we'd been sitting in. "What do you do for a living?"

"I work at an ar—" I stopped myself because the truth had almost slipped out, and she could never know the truth about me. "Art gallery," I filled in the blank. "As an office manager."

"Wow," she said with a dry laugh. "I never would've guessed that."

"Why do you say that?"

"You just don't seem like the artsy type."

I stared at her, probably for too long. She'd already *typed* me, as I had her. "And what type do you think I am?"

"I don't know," she said then laughed. She reached forward, pulling my straw toward her boldly and taking a sip of my drink, her pink lips enveloping the straw where mine had rested only moments ago. "I took you for something super smart and out of my league—like a doctor or a lawyer." She cringed. "Thank God you're not a dentist."

"Bad experience?" I laughed.

"Mouths freak me out."

I couldn't help it. My brows shot up, surprised and mildly put off by her comment. My mind was further in the gutter than a twelve-year-old boy. *Not all mouths, I hope.* She laughed as I thought it, as if she could read my mind, and I stared at her, my cheeks flaming with embarrassed heat.

"Sorry, that probably sounds bad," she said. Her laugh was warm and boisterous. It was nice, like a version of herself from the app sneaking through. She put a hand over her lips, her fingers touching the end of her nose. "I mean, I like what mouths can *do,* I'm just not a fan of seeing them be cleaned. My grandfather was a dentist before he retired. The stories he's told me..." She shivered, looking above our table at the air vent, though it wasn't on, and wrapped her arms around herself. "Sorry, probably not the sexiest first-date talk, is it?"

There was very little she could talk about that wouldn't be sexy, but teeth and oral hygiene did happen to top that list. I smirked.

"It's fine. Are you cold?" I shrugged off the bomber

jacket, handing it to her instinctually. It was what I would've done if Ainsley were there. I put a fist over my lips, then lowered it and took another drink, realizing it was the first time I'd thought of Ainsley in at least five minutes, and the thought of her hadn't sent a pang of guilt through me this time.

She took the jacket, wrapping it around her shoulders, and grinned up at me from behind thick lashes. It was as if I'd passed a test. She scooted further over on the bench toward the window and patted the seat beside her. "I'd be warmer if you were beside me."

I cleared my throat, watching her wanting eyes. She had the look of a woman who was not often told no. I'd never liked sitting side by side with someone while eating a meal. It wasn't comfortable or practical, but I refused to deny her request. Instead, I stood, watching the waiter approaching our booth. I slid next to her on the bench as he placed our plates in front of us.

"Is there anything else I can get for you guys?" If he found it odd to see two fully grown adults sitting on one side of the oversized bench, he hid it well. I felt the urge to lay my hands on the table in plain sight.

"I think we're good," Mallory said, and I felt her thigh pressing against mine.

"Okay, I'll be back to check on you soon." He tapped the table. "Enjoy." With that, he disappeared, and I began to unroll my silverware. Mallory's skin was pressed to my clothing at every joint—our elbows, our knees, our ankles—and she stared at her salad, then at me, a sly smile on her face.

"Better?" I asked, holding my fork in my hand as I

watched her. Every move she made was sensual, and I was sure she realized it, her fingers wrapped around the roll of silverware as she slid her hands down the length of the napkin before unrolling it.

"Much," she replied, popping a cherry tomato into her mouth.

My body pulsed with electricity, so full of excitement there was no longer room for hunger. I leaned back, wrapping one arm around her shoulders and lifting my drink to my lips. Her face glowed as she downed the rest of the whiskey in her glass and put a palm on my thigh.

I trembled at her touch, my throat dry, thoughts jumbled. "So, what do you do?" I asked, though I knew. I just needed something to fill the space. Replace the quiet with noise.

"I'm a massage therapist," she reminded me, her hand squeezing my thigh.

"That's right. Sorry, I forgot."

"It's okay. Easy to do." She didn't break eye contact, the food and drinks momentarily forgotten.

"Do you..." I took a deep breath, trying to slow my racing heart. "Do you like it?"

"Sometimes," she said, drawing the word out. She was even closer to me now, though I wasn't sure how that was possible. "Do you want to get out of here?"

My stomach flopped, a heavy pull coming from somewhere deep inside of me. "Out of here?"

"I'm not all that hungry anymore." Her eyes flicked down the length of my body and back up. "Not for food anyway."

I swallowed and nodded, standing up before she could

say another word. We needed to pay, but there was no check, no sign of the waiter, and no time to waste. I pulled out my wallet with shaking, impatient hands and tossed down three twenty-dollar bills, hoping it was enough, and took her hand as she led me out of the restaurant.

"I took an Uber. Did you drive?" she asked, nodding toward the street lined with parked cars.

"I'm in the parking garage," I told her, leading her in that direction. I couldn't stop my eyes from trailing down her body, wondering what was underneath the skintight dress and my oversized jacket. Not that her pictures had left much to the imagination.

"Can we go to your place?" she asked, making my blood run cold. "I have roommates."

"I, uh, I don't know," I said, trying to think on my feet. "I have kids." A version of the truth. When lying, you were supposed to go with a version of the truth, right? "They're home with a sitter, and I'd rather not bring someone— bring you—home, just in case they wake up."

"Kids, plural?"

"Three," I said with a laugh.

"Widower or divorced?" She seemed hesitant. Had I blown my chances?

Which was worse? "Divorced. Last year. I have joint custody."

"I'm sorry to hear that." I wasn't sure if she was talking about the kids or the divorce, so I nodded. "So, my place then?" she asked, recovering from her disappointment. She rolled her eyes and waved a hand nonchalantly. "Fine. Whatever. I've never brought a hot dad home. You'll be something new for my roommates to gossip about."

With that, she picked up the pace, heading toward the parking garage with me behind her. She led me to the elevator when I told her I'd parked on Floor 3, and we waited. When the doors opened, and then shut with us inside, she turned to me, her chest rising and falling with heavy breaths.

All at once, we lunged at each other. There was no other way to describe the way we moved together, our bodies smacking into one another. My lips found hers, the strong, acidic taste of whiskey on her tongue as it plunged into my mouth.

I didn't feel like I'd lost my footing as I'd been expecting to. Instead, my hand moved to her breast with ease. Our kiss grew more passionate, her expelling moans of pleasure as I spun us around, pressing her back to the metal wall of the elevator. The dinging noise of our arrival had us pulling apart, our lips red and swollen, stupid grins on both our faces.

We hurried toward my car, me leading the way this time, and climbed inside. Once there, we sat for a second, catching our breath from the kiss and the run and the excitement of the moment. I'd missed this feeling. God, I'd missed it. The uncertainty and the longing and the feeling like my chest was going to explode at any moment. The excitement in her eyes, the burning desire I knew we both felt. Where had it gone with Ainsley? Why had it fizzled out? Clearly, lacking passion was not my problem.

I started the car. "Where to?" Mallory leaned over, resting against my side as comfortably as she could over the center console. Her hand trailed between my legs, running up and down the seams of my pants as she gave me instructions, her floral-scented perfume so strong I was sure it would never come out of the fabric of my car or clothes. I could hardly think, and it was an absolute miracle that we made it out of downtown and to her neighborhood.

At one point, we nearly crashed as she took my hand and stuck it, without warning, inside her dress, my fingers cupping her bare breast. That was where it stayed, too, with no objection from me. My heart thudded so rapidly I was sure she could hear it; my palm sweating against her nipple for the entire rest of the ride. Her hips ground circles against the seat, her hand squeezing my inner thighs, working their way up to the bulge in my pants over and over again.

When we arrived, she instructed me to park across from a set of two-story townhomes, removed her hand from my lap, and adjusted the top of her dress as my hand left her breast.

She smiled at me, leaning over to kiss my lips before opening the door and stepping out. I stepped out of my side of the car, following her up the long walk to the red front door of the brick townhome.

"Shh," she cautioned. "I don't want to disturb my roommates." With that, she twisted the key in the lock and led us into the dark and silent living room. The home had the overwhelming scent of tacos and animal urine—not the most romantic combination. My stomach rolled from the stench, and I forced myself to breathe through my mouth.

She took my hand in the dark, making no effort to turn on a light, and led me down a hallway, past a set of closed doors, and up a tall, narrow staircase. I could hear the humming of a faint TV coming from one of the bedrooms and I wondered if her roommates were used to her sneaking random men into their home. At one point, she stumbled and laughed quietly, as if she were drunk, though I knew she hadn't had nearly enough to drink to be intoxicated in the slightest. We reached a door and she turned the handle, flipping on a lamp.

The room was average size and had a full-size bed against the far wall, with clothes draped across the end of it. There was a vanity to my left covered with makeup and perfume, bottles toppled over and powder everywhere. A small TV stand sat across from her bed, a stack of plates and empty cans of soda resting on its top. A laptop sat open, screen black, on the floor. Next to it, a navy blue dog bed sat, covered in long, white hair. I briefly wondered where the dog from her photos was.

It looked like a teenager's room, though much worse than my own teenager's. Ainsley would've had a fit if the kids' rooms were that messy.

I didn't need to think about that.

I didn't need to worry about a future with a woman who had no qualms about a lack of cleanliness. I didn't need to think about anything except the woman in front of me, unzipping her dress in slow motion. She let it fall away, revealing a tiny, matching set of lacy lingerie. She kicked the dress into the corner, pulling the clothes off the bed as I reached for the buttons of my shirt.

When she turned back to me, her eyes burned with the same desire I felt deep in my stomach. She reached for me, helping me with the last few buttons as her mouth found mine again.

Grabbing hold of my arms, she shoved me onto the bed and removed the last bit of fabric from her body. She stood in front of me for a few seconds, allowing me to take in the sight of her. Then, she leaned forward, pressing her lips to mine as she climbed onto the bed. I kissed her chest, her lips, her cheeks, her ears, unable to decide where to keep my mouth. Ending the struggle, she sat up, scooting one knee down the bed, then the other, working her way slowly toward my pelvis. She was an expert, practiced in the art of seduction. Every move she made somehow turned me on more.

I watched her unhook my belt, never breaking eye contact with me, her expression sultry and passionate. When she pulled my pants toward my ankles, she looked me over, a devilish grin on those pouty, pink lips, and I watched as her blonde head lowered, taking me into her mouth. The hair fell in front of her face, and I watched as it bobbed up and down, keeping a slow and steady pace.

I rested my head on the pillow, letting out haggard breaths as I watched her head—blonde, straight hair so starkly different from the red curls I was used to seeing there—as it moved up and down, coaxing strangled sounds from my throat. I was unable to control myself with her, and she seemed to be enjoying it.

In that moment, a moment of pure and seemingly unending ecstasy, I was so glad we did this. I was so grateful my wife had the idea. I was so glad I chose Mallory. I was so fucking glad I was there—

I couldn't think anymore. I needed to feel everything. I needed to be present.

I glanced down at the incredible view and thought about how lucky I was.

And then, as I felt the lightning tearing through my body, white-hot with pure pleasure as her eyes met mine again, I didn't think at all.

I just fucking felt.

CHAPTER NINE

AINSLEY

I was on the couch when I heard a noise outside and suspected it was Peter. When I glanced at the clock, an odd mixture of confusion and worry filled me. It wasn't even eight thirty, which means if he was back, the date either didn't go well or went *too* well and he had finished what he left the house to do.

Peter wasn't confident or outgoing, so I suspected it would be the former. He struggled with situations he wasn't comfortable in, yet thrived when he was comfortable. It was why his business had done so well, but he'd failed when trying to work for someone else. He didn't like to put himself out there for fear of rejection. He lived in his own head and got stressed out when things didn't go his way. He let the smallest things bother him, sitting with him and driving him crazy for weeks, sometimes months.

My husband was perpetually shy and calculating. He liked to plan and think things through. To put thought into his next move. He was the type to spend months reading reviews before buying a new coffee pot or obsess over and try on multiple coats from multiple stores before deciding on which he preferred. There was nothing spontaneous about him. It was why I'd been so surprised he'd agreed to the arrangement so easily. I thought I'd need to spend months selling him the idea before he agreed.

The noise came again, reminding me of what brought on my current train of thought, and I stood from the couch, listening to the steady pacing outside the door. There were no sounds of knocking. Only movement.

Surely he hadn't brought someone home with him. We'd never laid out that rule, but I'd assume he'd know it *was* one.

I peeked through the small glass window of the door, looking out onto the porch and sighed with relief. My best friend, Glennon, was there, her phone pressed to her ear. I swung open the door and looked out, and she placed her fingers over the microphone, smiling up at me joyfully as she mouthed, *"Sorry."*

"Okay, okay, Mom," she said, and I understood what was happening. "I will. Yep, love you too. Mmkay. Love you. Yep. Okay, bye."

She lowered the phone from her ear, rolling her eyes. "Sorry, my mom was telling me about her book club again. It's very scandalous there." Glennon leaned forward with a wink, wrapping her arms around me. "It's so good to see you, babe. Sorry it's unannounced. I'd planned to call on the way over, but you see how that turned out."

I stepped back, allowing her inside. "You never have to call, you know that. What are you doing out so late?"

"I wanted to check in. It's been a while since we hung out. Seth's at a work retreat thing." She sighed, taking off her coat and tossing it onto the coat rack next to the door. "I figured I'd come over and bother you and Peter for a while."

We walked into the kitchen together instinctually, our ritual whenever she came over. She grabbed the wine glasses while I pulled out the chardonnay. I preferred red, but the bottle had been opened a few nights ago and needed to be drunk. "Well, bother away. It's just me tonight. Hope that's okay."

"Where's Peter?" she asked over her shoulder, setting the glasses on the counter as I filled them and she wandered away to the pantry, which consisted of an entire room down the hall.

My answer was loud, meant to reach her there. "He's out. Work thing, I think." I hadn't told Glennon about what we were doing, though I'd always told her everything else, because I was embarrassed we'd even gotten to this point. Glennon and I were real with each other; we understood our respective marriages better than most counselors, but this felt like too much. When she returned to the room, she had a bag of caramel corn and one of cheddar popcorn.

"More snacks for me, then. Are we salty or sweet tonight?"

"Salty," I said with a laugh. "Always salty."

"Mm, you read my mind," she agreed, tossing the bag of caramel corn onto the countertop. "Speaking of *salty*, how are things? Got any salt to spill?"

I laughed. "I think you mean tea."

She wrinkled her nose. "Is that what the kids are calling it? I swear to God, I can't keep up anymore."

"Tell me about it. I need a translator to have a conversation with my three these days."

She chuckled. "Whatever. I feel like it's been a year and a half since I've seen you. How are you?"

"We got together for drinks last week," I pointed out.

"Much too long." She rolled her eyes playfully. "Speaking of the kiddos, where are they? Sleeping?"

"Well, they're supposed to be asleep, which means they're all up there playing on their phones like usual."

She walked toward me, taking the glass of wine as I held it out to her, her amber eyes locked with mine. "Is everything okay? You seem down."

The smile I gave her came on like a sneeze—quick and instinctual. It was a wall, meant to hide any form of worry or insecurity. "Everything's fine."

She knew better. "Fighting with Peter again?"

I shook my head. Glennon knew all about the fights, because all too often, it was her I ran to afterward. To vent, to cry, to weigh options when things were at their worst. It was Glennon who suggested the date nights and who pushed us to try therapy. Like a bossy older sister, she took the reins when my relationship began to go off course and tried to help bring us back someplace good.

"No, honestly," I told her, taking a sip of wine to cover whatever readable face I was sure I was making. "Everything's fine. What about you? How's Seth?"

Her smile was stymied by my words, falling to a flat line of thin lips. "Jesus, that bad? You can't even talk to me about it?"

I felt the heat rush to my cheeks, knowing there was no way around it. When I didn't say anything right away, she put her hands up. "Hey, no pressure, love. I won't force you. Just...you know I'm here, right?"

I was surprised to feel a lump forming in my throat, and I looked down, avoiding meeting her eye as I tried to collect myself. When I looked back up, I sniffled and nodded, and she took the hint, turning away. She opened the refrigerator and pulled out a second bottle of wine. "I think we're going to need this. I have *tea* to give you."

I smiled when she said it wrong, but didn't bother to correct her. It was far from my biggest problem. I hated feeling like I had to keep something so huge from her, but I couldn't tell her what we were up to. I wasn't ready. I hadn't figured out what to say.

"It's all about Seth's new assistant. Have I told you about her?" She wrinkled her nose in what looked like disgust. "Donna." I shook my head. With that, she let out a laugh and the conversation shifted easily, back to our usual banter. We headed into the living room and relaxed on the couch, sipping wine and bingeing terrible TV for the next several hours.

As the time passed, I realized it was the most fun I'd had in a long time. I always seemed to have more fun with Glennon than Peter. Maybe that was the problem. When was the last time I had fun with my husband?

CHAPTER TEN

PETER

W hen I got home that night, I was sure I reeked of sex. My hair was mussed, my clothing wrinkled, and I knew the guilt would tear away at my expression. How would I ever meet my wife's eyes again? I approached the door, surprised to see a light on in the living room. When I opened the door, there was stifled laughter that died out immediately.

Glennon was there. The last person I needed in my house right then. I wondered what Ainsley had told her about our arrangement. Hopefully nothing, probably everything. The agreement was that we wouldn't tell anyone, but those promises never seemed to include her best friend.

"Hey, honey," Ainsley said, her cheeks pink with wine, her tone slow and husky, as it often got when she'd had too much to drink. "Have fun?"

My own cheeks grew pink then, as my eyes darted from Glennon to Ainsley and then back. I didn't know what she knew, and I didn't want to deny it if she did know. *God, this is embarrassing.*

"Mhm," I said, deciding to get away as quickly as possible. I darted from the room and headed for the shower, my heart pounding with nerves and embarrassment. I heard them giggling again as I shut the door, and I realized what a fool I'd made of myself. As soon as the moment had passed, I felt the shame.

Like always.

That was how it happened. I'd always believed people assumed men were the ones who made the decision to cheat. That it was a conscious decision. Maybe for some men it could be, I didn't know. I hadn't exactly done the polling. For me, cheating on my wife had never been something I planned on. I wasn't proud of myself for what I'd done. Not that night or any of the nights before. And, to my surprise, it didn't feel any better now, just because I had permission.

The first time, it was a combination of bad timing—we'd had one of our worst fights that night—and too much alcohol. I'd wanted something to make me feel... something? Better, happier? *Anything.* I'd felt so numb in my marriage for so long. I loved my wife, but the love had faded. It was dulled by years of putting the children, the house, and our careers first. I needed to be reminded of what excitement felt like.

After it happened, as in *immediately* after, I swore it would never happen again. I felt sick. Disgusting. I hated myself. I couldn't bear to think about what I'd done. Like a murderer, I wandered through my life, waiting to be caught.

Every phone call, every text made me jumpy. I wondered would this be the call to end everything? Would this be the text where she would tell me she knew the truth? That she knew what I'd done? That it was time to face the music?

But the truth was, weeks went by and she never found out what I'd done. I'd gotten away with it.

In some ways, I wished I hadn't. Maybe that would've been better somehow. I would've been able to apologize. Maybe therapy would have fixed the one mistake. Instead, I got away with it and, when presented with another opportunity, I took it without a second thought. I ran with it, welcomed back into the warmth of the moment as if it were an old friend. It felt good. I'd missed it.

But the second it was over, the shit feeling from before was back. I hated myself even more, if that were possible. I was disgusted with who I was becoming. I thought there was no way I'd get away with it a second time. I thought she'd surely find out about it this time.

But she didn't.

Not the second time or the third. Not the fifth or the eighth or the tenth.

Eventually, I lost count as I made my way through the cycle. Each time, I thought—no, I swore—it would be the last time. I vowed I'd risked it too many times, and I never would again. And I believed it for a little while. But the wanting would always return. The opportunity would present itself, and I would jump at the chance to take it. And the guilt cycle would continue.

Now, even with permission, I'd fallen into the same set of steps I'd followed so many times before. First there was the shower, where I'd scrub my skin until it was red and raw, trying to scrub away any evidence, any trace that I'd done what I had. Then, I'd avoid her eyes, avoid her questions, and hope to get some sleep. Tomorrow, it would be easier, and each day after that even easier. But tonight would be hard, full of panic and worry—everything from STDs to pregnancy, but this time was different because I had one less thing to worry about. I didn't have to fret about Ainsley finding out. She already knew. She'd all but shoved me into Mallory's bed. So why didn't that knowledge make it easier on me? I wished I could understand it.

When I was done with my shower, and my skin was sufficiently red, raw, and scalding hot, I turned off the water, wrapped the towel around my waist, and ran a hand through my damp hair. There was less of it there than before; it was beginning to thin. Maybe not noticeably enough for someone else to realize it, but I knew it. The same way I knew my waist had begun to bulge over my pants ever so slightly. The way my legs burned a little extra when climbing the stairs and I found myself out of breath sooner. I was getting older. There was no denying it. My kids would remind me even if I tried to hide it.

I'd never been one to consider dyeing my hair. I'd always said I'd let the grays come as they did, but as they'd recently started coming in, I was starting to see the appeal. A box of brown dye could buy me a few more years. It was hard to deny the temptation. I made a mental note to look up reviews on brands when I had a moment at work.

I wiped the mirror dry and stared at myself. I still looked the same, despite the changes. I'd developed wrinkles by my eyes and on my forehead, but all in all, I was still the same guy. Wasn't I? How much had I changed, really?

Like that, I was wondering what Mallory thought of my performance that night. It was a shame she'd never know what I could do years ago, what I looked like then. It was unfortunate my best days were behind me, but I still liked to think I had a few good years left. A least a decade, right?

I turned away from the mirror and made my way across the room. When I opened the door, the cold air from the bedroom hit me, and I shivered. Ainsley was sitting in front of her vanity, running a brush through her long, red hair.

"Fun night?" she asked in a singsong voice.

"Looks like you're the one who had a fun night."

She giggled, placing her fingers in front of her lips. "I may have had an extra glass of wine or two."

"Or three or four," I murmured, pulling open my drawer and producing a clean pair of boxer briefs and pajama pants. I dropped the towel, turning away from her slightly as I pulled the clothes on. When I reached for the drawer again to search for a T-shirt, I felt her hands on my back.

I jolted, glancing over my shoulder at her. "*Jesus*, I didn't see you move."

She smiled, her eyes bloodshot. She *had* had a lot to drink. She trailed her fingers across my forearms, up my biceps, her gaze following her hands. She reached my neck, then my jawline.

"What are you doing?"

At my voice, her eyes flicked up to meet mine, batting

at me from behind her thick, dark lashes. "Appreciating my sexy husband. Is that not allowed?"

I swallowed, not sure when the last time she referred to me as *sexy* was, and gripped her waist, pressing our bodies together. It felt slightly wrong, after having just been with Mallory, but—

"Don't," she said, interrupting my thoughts.

"Don't what?"

"Don't think..." She pressed up onto her toes, kissing my lips. The kiss was soft at first, but then her lips parted and she sank into me, exhaling deeply. I felt the fire starting in the base of my stomach as she pulled the shirt from my hands and tossed it to the floor before running her fingernails down my back, then through my hair.

I inhaled her scent as I pushed her toward the bed. There was something different about her—wild and untamed, like how I remembered her from years ago. When we reached the bed, we broke apart and she untied the hot pink robe she was wearing and let it fall to the floor. Ordinarily, she'd be wearing a T-shirt and pajama shorts underneath, but that night, there was nothing. Nothing but her.

I took in the sight of her naked body. In recent years, we'd taken to having sex in the dark, usually under the covers. It was rare I was able to look at her like this, got to appreciate her like I was getting to now. I felt the heat traveling from my stomach, spreading throughout my limbs and appendages, filling me with desire. I leaned down, cupping her breast and pressing my lips to hers again.

For the first time in a long time as we moved together,

I couldn't seem to bring up a single thought. There was only her. I didn't worry. I didn't stress. I didn't think about work or the kids or the house or money. I just existed with her. I moved above her, within her. She took me in wholly, her eyes locked with mine. There was passion there that I hadn't seen from her in years, and though I had no idea what brought it on, I didn't care. I wanted her like I've never wanted anyone in my life.

Maybe her plan had worked after all.

CHAPTER ELEVEN

AINSLEY

P eter and I didn't talk most of the morning, though we were both still glowing from our night together. I didn't want to dissect what had happened, or why it happened, so I chose silence and he didn't press me for conversation. I was sure he was running through millions of questions in his mind too, but for the moment, it seemed best that we both sit with our thoughts and feelings until we knew what to do with them.

I dropped the kids off at school before heading toward the bank, my mind elsewhere. As I was driving, I heard my phone buzz from the cup holder and glanced down at the built-in screen on my dashboard.

2 New Dater Messages, it said, and I stared at the name, **Stefan.**

So, he hadn't given up yet. It was Friday, and all I wanted to do was make it through the day and to the weekend unscathed. But I knew the next week would bring a new set of challenges. I needed to connect with someone new by Tuesday. I needed to get the point across to Stefan, make him realize I wasn't going to respond, that I couldn't, and apparently that was going to be harder than I'd expected.

All too soon, I was at the bank and waiting on the all-clear signal from one of the bankers that said it was safe for us to go inside. When it arrived, a small slip of pre-agreed upon pink paper taped to the front door, I stepped from my car, grabbed the phone, my purse, and my tea, and headed toward the building.

Once I was inside, I glanced down at the screen, reading his message from within the app.

Checking in again. Can you at least let me know you're getting these?

The next one said, **I'm guessing I did something wrong—sorry about that. I told you I was rusty at this dating thing. Anyway, I wanted to apologize for whatever it is. You don't have to respond, but I had a lot of fun with you, and I hope I didn't offend you somehow. Have a great weekend, Ainsley. I hope you find what you're looking for.**

I nodded, lowering the phone as guilt and worry washed over me. *Poor Stefan. This wasn't what I wanted.*

"Good morning," I called to Brenda as she refilled the coffee pot on the far side of the lobby. I heard the clang of the vault door as the tellers opened it, beginning to remove their cash drawers and set up for the day. The building was eerily quiet for the most part, the sounds fresh and stunning in the stark silence. Before our customers arrived, before we opened our doors, it was always quiet. Most days, we were all still trying to wake up and get in our first few cups of coffee before the morning huddles and the craziness set in.

I put my key in the knob of my office door, twisted it, and froze, my body going icy. I grabbed the phone from my pocket again. *No.*

I reread the message. It wasn't possible.

No. No. No.

There it was. Why hadn't I caught it the first time? *Have a great weekend, Ainsley.* I sucked in a sharp breath, my arms lined with goose bumps as the question rang out in my head: *Why had he used my real name?*

CHAPTER TWELVE

PETER

I was on a call with a contractor when Gina stepped into my office. She walked forward and took a seat across from me, hands folded on her lap and one leg crossed over the other. The black fabric of her top stretched across her chest, and I watched as she leaned forward, rubbing a hand across her bare calf. When she met my eye, there was a mischievous look in her eye.

"Hello? Peter? Did I lose you?" the voice on the other end of the line called.

"Sorry, Jim. No, I'm here. And yes, that's fine. I can revise the blueprints to fit in the extra closet. Send me over the specifications, and I'll see about getting it approved by the end of next week."

"Excellent. I'll let the client know. Thanks."

"Talk soon." With that, I lowered the phone from my ear. I cleared my throat as I set it down, ending the call. "Sorry about that. Can I help you with something?"

"I'm hoping so." She smiled, and I wondered if her visit

was a business call after all. "I'm surprised you didn't text me."

I frowned. "I know. I'm sorry."

"You don't have to be sorry. I just wondered what the holdup was. Are you not interested anymore?"

"I-no, no, that's not it. I just...well," I ran my fingers through my hair awkwardly, "I don't want either of us to get hurt or...attached. You know. Because Ainsley and I are still trying to figure everything out. So, I guess I'm more or less looking for something fun and casual."

"And you don't think I'm fun and casual?" She blinked, her green eyes drilling me from behind the thick frames of her glasses.

"Well, I didn't say that. I was more worried I wouldn't be able to keep to the agreement. Seeing you every day... Anyway, I thought you said if I didn't text you, we'd never discuss this again?" I said, keeping my tone light. I hoped she would realize I was joking.

"Yeah, well, I guess I lied." She gave a dry laugh and leaned forward. "Come on, Peter, take me on one date. If you go back to your wife afterward, oh-fucking-well. I'm a big girl. I can handle rejection. I can handle fun and casual. What I can't handle is not even being given a chance." She paused, watching as I struggled with the decision. "Come on. We matched. That's a tangible social contract that you're breaking with zero regards for societal norms."

My hands went up in defeat, an easy smile playing on my lips. "Well, I can't break our social contract, now can I?"

"What kind of animal would you be?" she teased. I

chuckled, and she went on, "So, it's settled then? An official date is on the books?" She tucked a piece of hair behind her ears that had fallen loose from her low bun.

"An official date."

"Excellent." She smacked her lap, standing up. "When and where should I meet you?"

"Thursday at seven work for you?"

"Thursday, as in a week from now?" Her brows knitted together.

"No, Thursday as in six days from now."

She shook her head, not bothering to laugh at my joke. "That's too long. I'm free tonight. Meet me at Jonathan's at six." With that, she was out the door, and I had no time to object.

It was Friday, which meant there were no dates allowed and family time was firmly on the books. I had a choice to make. I stared at my computer, my mind racing, and jolted when my phone chimed. Her name stared back at me, with a **Can't wait** and a winking emoticon.

I sighed, and then, without any additional thought, I chose wrong.

CHAPTER THIRTEEN

AINSLEY

W hen my phone buzzed again, I was filled with dread. I'd spent all morning stressing about Stefan and trying to put it out of my head. After his message that morning, I was hoping he'd give up. I was clearly not going to respond to his messages, but in less than a week, I had received more than ten in total, so every time my phone went off, I'd begun to assume it would be him.

To my relief, it was only Peter.

I have to work late tonight. Can we reschedule family night?

I rolled my eyes and groaned. It was not a surprise. Peter had been working on two big projects at work, so I knew he was busy, but I'd hoped that night would be different. Especially given what had happened between us that morning.

I texted back a quick **Sure** and slid my phone into my desk drawer. I hated the way the disappointment sat with me. It was heavy, palatable. Like a meal I couldn't seem to rid myself of. It was the same feeling I had as a teenager before lowering my head over the toilet bowl and shoving my fingers down my throat. The action that gave me control over the feeling I hated so much. For the way I was feeling, no amount of purging would help. No amount of slicing of the skin of my inner thighs or running until my feet bled would solve this either, which were my other two coping mechanisms. I felt disgusting. Why had I let him do it to me again? Why had I allowed myself to hope things would be different? I hated feeling powerless. I thrived on fixing things and, when I had no way of doing so, it enraged me.

My phone buzzed, and I pulled it back out, wondering if he could tell I was mad, but the phone screen held Stefan's name again. I blew air from my lips, opening the app.

We need to talk. Please.

I tapped his picture, searching for a way to turn the notifications off. I didn't want to talk to him or anyone else at that moment. I was done talking. Why wasn't he getting it? Underneath his picture were three options.

Report

Block

Rate

I clicked the option to block him, and his picture disappeared. The screen changed to white, our messages gone. As if they'd never existed.

User Blocked.

There. I've done all I can do.

Now I just had to put the worry out of my mind and hope he'd gotten the message. Easier said than done.

CHAPTER FOURTEEN

PETER

I was at dinner with Gina, staring across the candlelit table at her, when my phone began to vibrate. I flipped it over on the table and stared at the screen. The groan escaped my throat before I had the chance to stop it.

Ainsley. What on earth could she want? We were only fifteen minutes into dinner.

"Everything okay?" Gina asked, leaning back from the table ever so slightly.

I nodded, considering ignoring the call. I didn't know what prompted me not to, but somehow I felt like I couldn't—that had never happened before. "I'm sorry. I need to take this. It'll just be a second." I held up a finger, lifting the phone to my ear as I rushed across the crowded restaurant and left my date alone. "Hey, is everything okay?"

Her response came in sharp, strained breaths. She was crying.

"Ainsley? What is it?" Concern swelled in my stomach.

Ainsley wasn't the type to cry easily. She didn't overreact or show emotion often, so if she was crying, something was wrong.

Again, I heard a sharp breath. "Someone's here." Her voice was low, a bit above a whisper. That was when I realized she wasn't crying after all. She was panicking. She was scared.

"What do you mean someone's there?"

"Someone's—" She was walking down the stairs then, I was almost positive. I heard her breathing grow labored, her voice echoing in the narrow hallway that led to our garage. "He won't leave."

"Who is it, Ains? Who's there?" I shoved my hand in my pocket, producing the keys from its depth and rushed back toward the table, no longer caring about anything other than getting home. Something was wrong, I could feel it in my gut, the worry burrowing itself in my bones.

"It's the guy I dated—Stefan. He—"

"Hang on. How did he find out where we live?"

"I have no idea," she shrieked. "Peter, I'm really scared. We messed up. We messed up so badly. He's stalking me, I think. He won't leave me alone. He keeps messaging me, and somehow he found out my real name, and now he's just shown up. Where are you? I don't know what to do. Please come home, Peter. Please."

"Okay, yes. I will. I'm coming home. Have you called the police?"

"*No!* No, it's more complicated than that. I don't know what he wants. I don't want everyone to know what's been going on. Please just get home and make him leave!

He'll back off if he sees you. I don't want the kids dragged into all of this."

"I hear you. I'm coming. Breathe, Ains, just breathe for me." Gina perked up as I reappeared in front of her, but I pulled the jacket off the back of the chair, offered a sorry expression, shook my head, and rushed away, then out the door. As I hit the sidewalk, I realized I'd left her with the bill and no explanation, but I had no time to worry about it. I needed to get home.

I slid into the car and pulled out of the parking lot. "I'm on my way, okay? Where are you now?"

"I'm in the hallway, trying to look out the window by the garage to see where he is."

"Where are the kids?"

"They went out," she whispered, sounding distracted. "Dylan's at Micah's, and Riley is working on a science project with Noah. Maisy went to Noelle's...or maybe Nicole's. I can't remember... Oh, wait... He may have left." She said it while expelling a sigh of relief. "I don't see him outside anywhere..."

"Okay, but I want you to stay where you are. Don't go looking for him. Wait until I can get there."

"I will," she promised. "Thank you for coming home. I'm sorry I interrupted you while you were working. I wouldn't have called if it wasn't important. I just got so freaked out."

I swallowed, trying to fight down the guilt I felt. I was supposed to be home. I should've been home. "You don't have to apologize for that. I'm glad you called." There was silence on the other end of the line, and I filled it by saying, "So, who is this guy?"

"His name's Stefan. He was the one I went out with Tuesday night. He's been contacting me quite a bit since then, and I was ignoring it. But earlier today, he called me by my real name, which I have no idea how he knows, but I thought maybe I slipped up somehow at dinner. So, I just blocked him in the app, and I thought that was the end of it. Then tonight, I heard a knock on the door and I walked over to answer it, and when I pulled it open, it was him. He didn't try to shove his way inside or anything. He said he wanted to talk. But... I was home alone, and I have no idea how he knows where I live or what he wants. I asked him to leave, but he kept arguing that we needed to talk, so I shut the door in his face and ran over here and called you."

Her voice was high and shaking, matching the frequency of my trembling hands on the wheel. Rage began to overtake the worry as I found myself fuming that someone was scaring my wife. That someone was bothering her. That he'd showed up at my house, where my kids live. Mostly, I was angry that I'd willingly put her in harm's way. I needed to fix this.

"I'm so glad the kids aren't here. I don't know what I'd do if they were here... What have we gotten ourselves into? We've put them in such danger."

"Do you think he's dangerous?"

"I don't know what to think. I didn't get that vibe on our date at all. He was sweet and...and...and normal. He's a widower, a bit older than us. He seemed, I don't know how else to describe it... He seemed *normal*. And, if he wanted to hurt me, he had the perfect opportunity. So why would he wait? Why would he do it like this?"

I shook my head. She was right—none of it made sense. What did he want? "I don't want to do this anymore," I blurted out.

"Don't want to do what?"

"Any of this. Seeing other people. I don't want to lose you. There are too many crazy people out there, Ains. I'd never forgive myself if something happened to you. If someone ever hurt you I'd—" I swallowed, stopping myself from finishing the sentence. I couldn't do it. I couldn't say the words. I was surprised to feel tears in my own eyes at the outright fear in my chest. I was terrified of losing her. I felt vulnerable in a way I hadn't in years. How would I go on without her if something ever happened?

She was quiet for a moment before saying, "I agree."

"You do?" I didn't know why it shocked me so much, but there was no denying the stupor I felt at her words.

Instead of answering, she remained quiet. I pressed on. "Ainsley?"

"He's...still...here." Her words came slowly, their essence barely audible. I could hardly understand her, but I knew what she'd said. I pressed the accelerator, jolting the car forward, my chest tight.

"Okay...is he in the house?"

Silence.

"Ainsley, I want you to stay on the line with me, okay? Get somewhere. Get in a room, a closet, and stay with me, okay?" I begged her to answer, to let me know she was safe, but she remained silent. I could hear her slow and haggard breathing through the line. She was still there. Still alive. I just needed to keep her that way. "I'm coming.

I'm coming as fast as I can. Hang on, okay?" The smart thing to do, I knew, would be to call the police, but I couldn't bring myself to end the call. I needed to keep her on the line. I was crying at that point—silent, helpless tears escaping my eyes and blurring my vision. I focused on the sounds of her breathing, loud over the Bluetooth system in the car, and remained silent the rest of the way.

Twenty minutes later, I turned into and drove down our long, forest-lined driveway. I'd always loved living on our own land, far away from the nearest neighbors, but at that moment, I regretted the decision.

"I'm here," I whispered, and her breath came in the form of a sigh of relief. A beat-up red truck sat in the driveway, its engine shut off. Was he inside the truck? Would he come after me? "Can you tell me where he is?" I looked toward the front door, the porch light off, searching the shadows. It was too dark to make out if anyone was there.

"The...porch. The...bat..." At her words, I hurried to the trunk and pulled out the metal baseball bat I'd carried since college, ended the call, and walked toward the front porch. I left the trunk and car door open, taking quiet footsteps across the gravel. As I neared the porch, conscious of my too-loud breathing, I was able to make out the dark figure that awaited me. He was facing the door, and as I got closer, he knocked on it loudly.

"Ainsley," he called. "Open the door!"

I took another step forward, the wood of the porch squeaking under my weight, and he spun around.

"Who're you?" the cold, deep voice demanded.

"You need to leave," I said, fighting to keep my voice

from shaking. I wiggled the bat in the air, a warning to him. "I don't know how you found out where we live, but you need to leave."

"Not until I see Ainsley. And put that bat down before you hurt yourself."

His words sent chills down my arms as he stepped forward, and I was able to somewhat make out his face in the moonlight. He was bald, with sharp features and a stocky build. He kept his shoulders squared to me as he moved closer, and I stepped back.

"Who are you?" I asked, keeping the bat resting on my shoulder. "What do you want with her?"

"You must be the husband?" he asked, his voice dry, almost sarcastic.

"I am, yeah. *Who are you? What the hell are you doing here?"*

He let out a chuckle. "Listen, man, I know she's here. I want to see her. That's all. Open the door, and no one has to get hurt. And, for the last time, *lower the bat."* He didn't seem at all concerned that I was standing there, bat in hand, ready to attack. He stood, hands in his pockets, as if he didn't have a care in the world.

I growled, wiggling it. "I'm going to call the police if you don't get the hell out of here now."

"Good luck with that," he said, pulling his hands out of his pockets and raising his knuckles to the glass of the door. He rapped on it loudly. "Ainsley! It's me. It's Stefan. Come on. Open up!"

"I'm giving you one last chance to get out of here, or else I'll—"

"You'll what? What are you going to do, tough guy?"

He spun around, his hands resting on his waist, where I saw the outline of a gun. Chills ran across my skin at the sight. "You think you're some big shot, don't you? Let me tell you something, fucker, you make a move to lay a finger on me, and I'll have you on your back before you know what hit you. So I suggest you do what I say, take a step back, and think about what you're about to do—"

"Please don't hurt him!" The front door swung open, and I heard her squeal. As she did, he lunged for her, both arms outstretched as he stepped toward the open door. I swung the bat, making contact with his head in one swift motion, and his head bounced off the exterior wall before he tumbled to the ground. He rolled over quickly, reaching for his gun, but he was clearly disoriented and I had the upper hand. I swung again, fury radiating through me as I made contact with his skull again.

Over Ainsley's cries, I heard the sickening sound of the metal bat connecting with his thick skull. It was a crunch I was sure I'd never forget. His hands twitched once more, and I swung a third time. This time, the night fell silent. Ainsley's cries stopped. The only thing left to hear was my own breathing, heavy and rattled.

"Peter, what did you do?" she asked, her shaking voice carrying across the dark porch. I put my hands over my mouth, feeling vomit rising in my throat as the scent of blood reached my nose. I hurried across the porch, barely making it to the edge before I began to spew the drink I'd had at dinner. It burned my throat and nostrils, my vision blurring with tears as I heard her cry out from behind me.

What did you do? she asked again, though I was in no position to answer her. When the retching ended, I turned back around, dropping the bat that I still held in my hand and staring at the body in horror. She flipped on the porch light, giving us a better view of the mess I'd made. His skull had cracked open, blood spilling out across the porch in every direction. "Oh, Peter. Oh, no!" she cried, staring at me, then the body, then back to me. "How could you?"

"He was trying to hurt you," I said breathily, wiping my mouth with the back of my hand. "I-I had no choice."

She stared at him in horror, shaking her head with her palm firmly over her mouth. She was fighting back tears as she spoke again. "Oh my God. What do we do? *What do we do?* The kids will be home soon! We have to move him, Peter. They can't see this! The kids can't see this! We have to call the police! *We have to do something!*"

"Are you kidding? We…we can't call the police. Look at him. Look at what I did. They'll arrest me—"

"He was trespassing! He had a gun! *He was going to shoot you! He was going to kill us both.*"

I slapped my forehead, rubbing the sweat from my temple as I tried to think. I'd killed him. I'd done it. He was dead. The kids would be home soon. If we were caught, I'd go to prison. If Ainsley called the police, I'd go to prison. Would the police believe me? I stepped forward, looking for the gun again to be sure I'd seen correctly. As long as it was there, maybe I'd stand a chance. When I saw it, there in his hand like I expected it to be, I swallowed. Next to the holster where it had been, hung a pair of silver handcuffs.

"*What the hell?*" I moved even closer, looking the body over. He was dressed in jeans and a long sleeved navy blue shirt, now spattered with blood, but at his waist, he wore a tactical belt, a gun holster, and what appeared to be high-quality handcuffs. "Is this guy a cop, Ainsley?" I pointed, but she'd seen what I had.

"I-I don't-I didn't—"

"Is he?" I demanded. My heart was pounding so ferociously in my chest I could hear nothing else. My vision blurred at the edges as I looked back out at the driveway. He'd come in a red Toyota truck, not a cop car, but if he was off-duty that wouldn't matter, would it? "Check his pockets..." She shook her head, unmoving. "We have to do it," I said.

"You do it, then."

I gritted my teeth, moving toward him cautiously. Though I knew it would be impossible, I kept waiting for him to reach out and grab my leg. I bent down, sticking my hand in his back pocket and pulling out a wallet. I opened it, staring at the photo ID long enough to catch his name and address: Stefan De Luca of 118 Roberts Drive. He hadn't lived far from us. Just across town. I shuddered as the thought rolled over me. A flap of leather covered his cards, and when I flipped it over, I dropped the wallet. The golden badge shone up at us in the glare of the porch light.

"Shit, shit, shit, shit..." I paced the porch, pounding my hand into my forehead as I tried to think. "Fuck, Ainsley! *What do we do?* What did you do?"

"Peter, I swear to you, I had no idea he was a cop. He didn't tell me that. We didn't talk about our careers. Maybe it's a fake badge. I don't know... We didn't talk that much... I barely know him..." she trailed off, her voice breathy and shaking. "What do we do?" She was trembling, both her body and her voice, and when I turned to face her, she wouldn't meet my eyes. She kept staring at the body in horror. I couldn't bring myself to look as my stomach continued to rumble.

"We can't call the police and tell them I killed a cop, Ainsley. There's no way I'm getting off after that. We have to get rid of the body," I told her in a moment of stunning clarity. "It's all there is to do. We have to make it look like he was never here, and then we pretend like this night never happened."

"How can you say that? How can we possibly do that? We don't know the first thing about cleaning up a dead body."

"We're going to have to figure it out," I said. "It's our only choice."

"But..."

"Come on," I begged her, "*please.* We have to get rid of the body and his truck. It's the only way."

"It's tampering with evidence—"

"It's *fucking murder,* Ainsley. We can't chance it. We can do this, okay? We can clean it up. We can fix this. You're always saying you're the fixer, right? So you have to fix this, babe. You have to." I watched as she contemplated what I was saying, hoping and praying she'd agree with me. We couldn't call the cops. It was too much of a risk. To my relief, when she looked up at me again, she nodded, wiping her hair out of her face as she accepted the assignment. She breathed out a heavy breath from her O-shaped lips. "You're right. It's...it's the only way. Let me think for a minute."

I paced the porch, watching her as she tapped her fingers on her lips, formulating a plan I wasn't yet allowed to know. After a few moments, a familiar look filled her face. She'd figured it out. Everything was going to be all right.

CHAPTER FIFTEEN

AINSLEY

W e'd debated back and forth about where to put the body—try and find some place to dump it, bury it in the backyard, bury it in the woods, take Stefan's truck and leave it somewhere with the body inside—but in the end, we decided leaving the house was too much of a risk.

I'd had Peter remove a piece of the lattice board that framed our elevated, wraparound porch and crawled underneath. It hadn't been easy, the crawl space was maybe three feet tall, so getting the shovel under the porch and using it to dig a hole several feet under the ground was grueling and time-consuming. Once he had the body under the porch, I'd taken Stefan's cell phone, loaded up into his truck, and driven across town while my phone remained at home. I pulled into the airport and dropped it off without paying for a spot. Next, I turned off his phone, wiped it clean of my prints, and tucked it under the seat. Once Peter had the body, wallet, and gun buried, he met me at the airport, picked me up at our agreed upon location, and we drove home in silence. I didn't ask him what he'd done or how it had gone. I simply sat with my terrified thoughts and worried about what would happen to us. Though Peter had been the murderer, I was now an accomplice. I'd hidden evidence. I'd broken the law. If one of us went down, the other would, too. So, we just had to make sure neither of us did. That was the unspoken agreement—we were in this together.

When we'd arrived at home, I'd come inside to wash myself up while he scrubbed the porch. I couldn't get the blood out from under my fingernails no matter how hard I scrubbed. I continued to find flecks of red hidden in cracks and crevices of my skin and cuticles.

After several minutes passed, Peter walked back into the bathroom, and I shut the water off, staring at the bucket in his hand. He smelled of pure bleach, his skin pale despite the dirt smears across his forehead and under his nose.

I stared at him, my head feeling foggy and out of sorts. "Is it cleaned up?"

He nodded, his Adam's apple bobbing. He couldn't speak, couldn't look me in the eye. It was too awful. Too terrible, what we'd done. Now the body was buried, the blood from the porch had been cleaned up, and all that was left to get rid of was our clothes and any remaining evidence before the kids got home, which would be at literally any moment. As I stared at him, he walked across the bathroom floor and dumped the bucket of bleach into the tub. The liquid was tinged red, the yellow sponge in his hand an odd shade of orange.

"Do you want to double check that he's...deep enough?" he asked, his voice powerless.

"No. I can't bear to go out there again. I'll just have to trust you. Take off your clothes," I told him, holding out my hand. Without question, he did as he was instructed, stripping down and handing them over to me. He climbed in the shower, turning on the water as I pulled my own clothes off and gathered them up. I wrapped a robe around myself and hurried to the laundry room, where I dumped the clothes into the washer, turned it on the hottest setting, dumped in five times the stain remover than what was needed, added the remainder of the bleach, and turned it on. I closed the lid, listening to the water kick on. As it did, I rested my back against the washing machine, sinking down to the ground as the reality of what we'd done crashed into me, my adrenaline fading for the first time all night.

My hands shook, but I squeezed them together, digging my fingernails into my palms. I needed to pull myself together. I couldn't lose it. I shut my mind off, falling deeper into myself as I did when I meditated. Nothing else existed. Just me and the sound of my breathing. I felt my heart rate slow almost instantly, reopening my eyes with a sudden sense of calm. I sat, listening to the washing machine washing away the last bit of evidence of what we'd done.

Minutes passed, hours maybe, before I heard the front door open, and I gasped. I stood up, dusting myself off and tightening the robe around my waist. I glanced at the washer once before rushing down the hall and toward the living room. As I went, I spotted another speck of blood under my thumbnail. I shoved my hands into the over-sized pockets of the robe.

"Mom!" Dylan cried, his voice carrying through the quiet house.

"What is it?" I rushed toward him, my voice shrill and panicked. What had he seen? Had we missed something?

"What's going on? What's wrong?" he asked, his dark brows knitted together.

"Nothing's the matter. What do you mean?" I asked, trying to stop my body from jittering as I reached him.

"You look like you're going to be sick. And what's going on with the porch?"

A weight dropped in my stomach. "What's wrong with the porch?"

"There's a piece of the white stuff that goes on the bottom of it lying in the yard, for starters," he said with a laugh. "And it smells like straight bleach out there."

I inhaled, my eyes darting between his. How could Peter have been so stupid not to put the lattice back? I put my hands on Dylan's shoulders, and he looked at me as if I'd suddenly stood on my head, glancing down at my hands in pure horror. "Something is wrong, isn't it? Did someone get hurt? Is it Dad? Is someone sick?"

"Yes," I answered, forming my thoughts as I spoke. "I'm sick…Just a bit of a stomach bug, but I got sick outside on the porch, and your father and I had to clean it up. I'm sorry if we worried you."

He looked me up and down, concern filling his expression. "Oh, that's all? Well, are you going to be okay?"

I nodded. "I'm fine, sweetheart. Why don't you go on

to your room? I don't want to risk giving it to you or your brother or sister if I can avoid it."

He took a step away from me, but it was hesitant. "Are you sure you're okay? You don't look very good."

"I'm fine," I repeated, placing my hand on my stomach this time for good measure. "Just a bug I caught at work. You ate, right?"

"Yeah, yeah," he said, taking another step away from me. "Where's Dad?"

"He's taking a shower," I told him. Just as I heard the bathroom door down the hall open, Peter's heavy footsteps headed in our direction. "Honey, Dylan's home."

"Hey, son!" he called, much too enthusiastically. I hoped I didn't sound as guilty as he did.

"Go on to your room, okay? I don't want you to catch whatever this is." I touched his shoulder again, dismissing him and watching as he disappeared down the dark hallway. Seconds later, Peter appeared, his face ashen and distressed.

"What did you do with the clothes?" he asked.

"They're in the wash."

He nodded.

I lowered my voice and stepped a bit closer. "I'm going to take my shower. You need to put the lattice back. You left it lying in the yard."

He cursed under his breath. "I was waiting to put it back until I gave you a chance to double-check that I'd done everything okay. Did Dylan notice?"

"He's the one who told me. Not only did *he* notice, but I'm sure Micah's parents did too when they dropped him off. You could've at least set it back in place. You knew any of the kids could've come home at any moment. How could you be so stupid?"

He stalked past me, refusing to argue, and slammed the front door behind him. I sighed, already amped up for a fight, but gave up, heading down the hall myself. I needed to wash away all evidence of our night. I needed to sink into the darkness again.

CHAPTER SIXTEEN

PETER

It was my worst nightmare, living with what we'd done. I tossed and turned the entire night, replaying the evening's events over and over in my head.

The day had started out so normal; how had things gone so wrong? How would I ever sleep again knowing the evidence that I was a murderer was buried just outside? That anyone could find it at any time? Every night for the rest of my life, every single day, I'd be reminded that I was a killer. That I'd killed a man. That I'd killed a *cop*. That I'd killed a cop in front of my wife.

She'd never forget it. She'd never unsee what I'd done. She must've hated me. How had I let us get here? Why had I ever let her go out with that monster? How would I ever be able to breathe again? How would we survive this?

There was a time when I was sure my secret about the other women would destroy me, but this was so much worse. That was an eyelash stuck in the corner of my eye, mildly painful and obtrusive, annoying as all hell, but I could live with it. And I had. This…the fact that Ainsley had watched me become a monster before her very eyes, the fact that there was a dead body buried just outside our front door...it was a scalding hot poker to my insides, the scraping and pulling of all my muscles in opposite directions. It burned and stung and made it impossible to breathe, impossible to think of anything else.

How would I continue living? The idea of going to work on Monday, of facing coworkers, facing my children, while I had no control over who might come snooping around, what wild animal might catch the scent on the wind and dig up the body... It was too much to bear. I couldn't go to prison. I needed to be here for my kids. I needed to be here for my wife.

I rolled over for the eightieth time, pulling the covers out from under my side. When I looked to Ainsley's side of the bed, I jumped, sucking in a breath. She was lying there, awake, eyes open and staring straight at me. She had a determined look in her eyes I knew well.

"You need to calm down," she said softly, her tone firm.

"How am I supposed to be calm right now?" I asked. "How are you calm?"

"I'm not calm," she said, "but I know that if we don't at least *seem* calm, we're going to get caught."

"What did you do with the...er, the bat?"

"I bleached it. Tomorrow, I'll take it with me on my way to work and drop it in a dumpster downtown."

"Do you think it's okay to leave...him...where he is? Will he start to...stink or—"

"We don't have a choice right now," she cut me off.

"He's there, and for all we know, that's okay. You think he's down deep enough, right? To hide the smell?"

"How should I know?" I asked, my hands shaking again. "It's not like I have any experience digging graves to know how deep the bodies should be buried."

"Did you bury him deeper than you buried Scout?"

The kids' beloved German Shepard that had died two years ago. I swallowed at the thought. That day was painful. This day was unbearable.

"I think so. Maybe. At least as deep. A few feet."

She sighed, displeased with my answer.

"It'll have to do for now."

"What will we tell the police if they come asking questions? What am I supposed to tell Gina about why I left the...er...the meeting?"

Her eyes narrowed at me slightly. "Tell Gina, or Beckman, or anyone else that I got sick and needed you to come home. And why would the police come around asking questions here?"

"Well, he was your date, wasn't he? There've been conversations between you two. Won't they come around and ask you how you knew him and if you've seen him recently?"

"I used a fake identity on the app, Peter. That was the whole point."

I scoffed. How did she seem so calm? It was driving me crazy. I kept seeing flashes of the blood, wondering if we'd managed to wipe away every spot of evidence, and she looked like it was just another Friday night. "Yeah, but they'll be able to find you still, right? You said he used your real name on the app, so he obviously knew who you were. Like you said, maybe you slipped up, but he had our address either way. And the police will have your IP address or whatever. They'll connect the dots back to you."

"He only used my name once, and not even my last name. However he figured out who I was, surely he covered his tracks, right? I don't think cops can just *stalk* people for no reason. Besides, the app's privacy guarantee is super strict. They don't store IP addresses or anything aside from what you put on your profile. Remember? They were the ones who got in all that trouble last year because the police were trying to investigate a girl who was attacked and the company had no information on whom she'd gone on dates with other than his profile, which was obviously fake. It was all over the news. They guarantee privacy, and they stood by that in court. I mean, it was awful, but it's part of the reason I chose that app for us to use. I didn't want anyone to be able to find us. Those computer geniuses...they could probably track us down if they wanted to. I didn't want to chance it. You don't remember hearing about that case?"

"What?" I asked, feeling a strange mixture of shock and disgust. "I mean, of course I remember hearing about it, but I didn't remember the name of the app. Why would you ever want to use it? Do you have any idea how dangerous that was?"

"Well, you should be glad I did because it may be the only thing standing in the way of you going to prison." My face fell as I stared into her hardened expression. After a moment, it softened. "I'm sorry, I didn't mean that. I'm just stressed out."

"I am too," I whispered, rubbing my hands over her arms. "Trust me, I am. I'm so sorry I put us in this situation."

"You were trying to protect us," she said softly, but I sensed the disappointment in her tone.

"I'm still sorry. If it comes down to it, you know I'll take the blame." I reached for her hand, taking her fingers in mine and rubbing them between my thumb and fingers.

"It's both of our faults. I should've never suggested we see other people. This whole thing was my idea. If anyone's to blame, it's me." She said it plainly, leaving no room for negotiation, but I could sense the vulnerability there.

"Don't say that. None of this is your fault. He was a bad man who wanted to hurt you. He must've looked into you. Like you said, he'd been stalking you. Harassing you. Messaging you all the time. He showed up at our house... That was all on him."

"What do you think he wanted?" she asked, dropping her head a bit and tucking her chin to her chest. "Why do you think he wouldn't leave me alone? Do you think he was planning to hurt me?"

"I don't know," I said, resisting the sudden urge to pull her to my chest and comfort her. "He said he wanted to see you. He threatened me. He said if I didn't put my bat away someone was going to get hurt and, when you opened the door, he was going to grab you... I knew he had the gun. He could've held you hostage. I just...I snapped. I couldn't let him hurt you. Why else would he have brought his weapon and handcuffs? It doesn't make any sense."

"How did he even find me, though? How did he learn my real name? I was so careful. I truly don't think I would've slipped up that badly," she insisted.

I shook my head. "I don't know... I mean, he was a cop. Maybe he ran your plates? Maybe he saw your ID when you ordered a drink. There are probably a million ways he could've found out who you were... We could try to look him up—"

"No," she said. "We can't. We can't give anyone any further reason to look into us. We need to forget about it."

"Should we delete the app?"

"Not yet," she said. "If the police were to come looking for me, it might seem suspicious. There's nothing incriminating in our messages. If anything, there's proof that he was stalking me. We'll leave the app on our phones for now, but we're both in agreement that we don't connect with anyone else on there. We're done with this...arrangement."

I nodded. "Okay, agreed."

She shivered. "I'm so sorry about all of this. I don't understand how it happened. It all feels like a flash. I was so scared... I didn't know what to do. I should've told you about him before, but I was nervous. I didn't want to break any of our rules, and I didn't want you to obsess over who he was. I never, in a million years, thought he could be dangerous. He seemed so sweet on our date. I never thought... How did I misread him so badly?"

"I'd say he had a lot of practice hiding who he was." I slid my hand from her arm to her waist, gripping it

tightly. "I don't know what I would've done if I'd lost you. I'm sorry I wasn't here."

"It wasn't your fault you had to work," she whispered.

"Yeah." I swallowed, the bitter truth sitting on the tip of my tongue. I wanted to tell her about Gina. I didn't want to lie to her, but the truth at that moment wouldn't do anyone any good. "Well, no more late nights. I want to fix us, Ainsley. I want us to be better than we've ever been. I almost lost you tonight... I never want to lose, or almost-lose, you again."

Her smile was small, her eyes exhausted. "I love you."

"I love you too," I swore to her, squeezing my eyes to hide the tears I felt preparing to fall. I tucked my face into my pillow and sucked in a breath. My mistakes, countless and longstanding, were what had brought us to this moment. If I hadn't been distancing myself because I was cheating, we wouldn't have needed the arrangement in the first place. If I hadn't lied about my whereabouts tonight, I would've known what was going on and perhaps been able to prepare myself or call the police. Everything could've gone so much differently, if only I'd been a better man.

But I was vowing then and there to become better. I'd put the night behind me and make myself the man my wife deserved.

If only it were that easy.

CHAPTER SEVENTEEN

AINSLEY

As I headed into work that Saturday morning, leaving Peter at home with the kids, I checked the rearview mirror incessantly, my stomach going tight each and every time I passed a cop car. When I arrived downtown, it was still early, the streets slow and uncrowded, businesses just beginning their days. I drove through the familiar streets, searching for an unmanned dumpster. I spotted one, between a Subway and a coffee shop, and pulled my car to a stop in the alley. I'd brought a few random things from the garage to make it look less suspicious.

I stepped from the car, pulling on a jacket and flipping up the hood. It wouldn't look strange on the cool, crisp morning to be wearing a hood, so it was an added bonus that it could help to conceal my identity from any nearby cameras. I rubbed my hands together as I made my way toward the trunk, pulling out a bag of clothes the kids had outgrown, a box from an Amazon package that had arrived a few weeks ago—shipping label removed—a baby bath we'd had sitting in the garage for years, and the freshly bleached bat. I carried them all under my arms as I made my way toward the dumpster, checking my surroundings every few steps.

A few people walked past, not paying me any attention as they made their way toward their destinations—some on phones, some sipping coffees, some with headphones on—oblivious to anything else happening around them.

The alley was wide, littered with old, broken pallets and wet boxes. I scurried toward it, ignoring the sign that said it was for North End Property tenants only, and dumped the items in among black bags of garbage and empty boxes from soda syrup. I heaved a sigh, rubbing my hands together to warm them and adjusting the items so they covered the bat.

When I turned around, to my relief, no one was there to see what I'd done. I walked away, trying to ease the worry that had grown in me. The second I left the bat, I knew, it would be out of my control. Anyone could find it. Anyone could turn it in. But to keep it at our house or in our cars seemed like even more of a risk. It was too dangerous. I continued to walk back to my car, feeling sick to my stomach. I cut off an elderly couple on their way down the sidewalk, arms locked together as they talked in hushed tones.

"Sorry," I apologized, holding up a hand. I tucked my chin to my chest and walked quicker, my hands trembling as I pulled out my keys, unlocked the doors, and started the car. I flipped on the heat, rubbing my hands together once more as I tried to still my tremor-ridden, adrenaline-filled body.

As I pulled out onto the street, my phone began to ring, causing me to hold my breath as I waited for the caller's name to fill the screen on my dashboard. When I saw it was only Glennon, I released the breath and pressed the button on my steering wheel to answer the call.

"Hello?"

"Hey, love, what are you doing today?"

"I'm on my way to work this morning. Why?"

"I was just checking in on you. I thought maybe you could use some company. You're off at noon, right?"

"Around then, yeah," I said, thinking quickly. I wished that the only secret I had to keep from my best friend was that Peter and I had tried an open marriage briefly. The newest secret was so much bigger and would be so much more difficult to keep. Glennon could read me like a book, she always had been able to, so I needed more time to get the lies in order before I could see her.

"Great. Wanna meet for coffee after that?"

"I'd love to, but I can't. I've got something planned with Peter and the kids."

"Ooh, fun! What are you doing?"

"We're going to attempt family pictures," I said with a forced laugh.

"That'll be so nice, babe! How long has it been since you had pictures? Maisy was a baby, right?"

"Yeah, basically." The genuine excitement for us in her tone was killing me. "I'm not sure how it'll go, but that's the plan."

"Are you doing a whole tripod-in-the-yard thing? Need a photographer? My rates are good," she teased.

"No, we've got one. But thanks for the offer." I kept my tone cool and light. "One of Peter's coworkers has a daughter who's started her own photography company. We're going to give her a shot, help her get some experience. She's super affordable, so if it goes well, I'll give you her info in case you and Seth want to try her out."

"Oh, fun. I love it. I can't wait to see them."

"Thanks, yeah, you know I'll send some your way."

"Thanks, love..." She was quiet. I knew there was something else she wanted to say.

"You okay?"

"Mhm, everything's fine. Sorry, I zoned out there for a minute. Okay, well, I'll see you later then. Have fun at work."

"Hey, wait!" I called, trying to stop her from hanging up.

"Yeah?"

"Are you sure you're okay? Is something wrong?"

"Nah," she said, her voice a low growl, as if she'd recently woken up. "I'm fine. I just wanted to call and check in."

"I miss you," I said, though I had no idea why. I needed to keep her away, not give her further reasons to come by.

"I miss you, too. I'll see you soon though, right?"

"Maybe we can hang out after work one night this week." Another cop car passed me, this one with its lights on, siren blaring. My throat felt tight as it flew past me. Moments later, I turned onto my branch's street.

"Yeah, sounds good."

"All right, well, I'm almost at work, so I guess I'll talk to you later."

"Yep, later, love." She ended the call before I'd had time to say goodbye.

How strange.

But I had no time for deciphering my best friend because at the moment, my hands were quite full concealing a murder. As I pulled into the parking lot, my blood went cold. I shook my head, though no one was there to see.

No. No. No. No.

The parking lot had two police cars in it, parked directly in front of the door, lights flashing.

Had we been caught?

CHAPTER EIGHTEEN

PETER

After Ainsley left for work, I got out of bed and headed downstairs to make a pot of coffee. As much as I felt like lying in bed all day, I knew I needed to get outside and check the porch in the daylight to be sure we hadn't missed anything the night before. Ainsley had left through the garage, and I hadn't had the heart to put anything else on her; she was already in charge of disposing of the murder weapon. The least I could do was check to make sure we'd cleaned up the rest of the evidence.

Though I wanted nothing more than to stay in bed and pretend the day before hadn't happened, I had to get up and moving. I knew the kids would all sleep past noon, but I didn't want to take any chances on visitors or anything of the sort.

Before I'd brushed my teeth or gotten dressed, I made my way through the house and opened the front door. I looked down, glad to see the paint hadn't been removed by the massive amounts of bleach, but, like I'd feared, there was a definite ring of brighter paint just in front of the door. It was obvious we'd cleaned something there. I needed to wipe down the entire area. And fast.

I rushed inside, filled the bucket with bleach and water, and headed back outside with a mop. I set to work, swiping from top to bottom, the smell of the bleach making me nauseous. It was a startling reminder of the night before, making me jittery and nervous again. I couldn't help looking through the razor-thin gaps in the porch, knowing what, or rather *who*, lay below.

Once the entire porch had been cleaned, I stepped back, looking over my work. It looked much better. No longer could you see the circle where I'd scrubbed until it was two shades brighter than the rest of the dirty porch.

As I heard a car pulling in the driveway, I looked up, surprised to see Glennon's SUV pulling in. I groaned, setting the mop back into the bucket and crossing my arms as she climbed from the vehicle and stepped out onto the drive, headed my way with two red coffee cups in her hand.

"Got your favorite," she called.

"Thanks. Ainsley isn't here," I told her, though I suspected she knew that because she'd only brought two drinks with her, and presumably one was for herself.

"I know. I called her on the way to work, and she said she was at the office today. I wanted to come by and see if you needed any help preparing for the pictures."

My brow furrowed. "Pictures?"

She nodded. "Family pictures…today. Ainsley said you all were doing pictures, right?"

I sucked in a breath, angry Ainsley hadn't prepared me for the lie, and nodded, scratching my temple. "Yeah, that's right. Shit. I almost forgot." I took the cup of coffee from her, its warmth spreading throughout my body.

She studied me. "She said you're planning to use a tripod, so I thought I could come over and help you set up or help get the kids ready, or whatever you might need."

"Yeah," I said, nodding as I tried to keep up. "Er, I mean, no. I think we're okay. Ainsley hasn't told me what we're even wearing yet. I assume she'll figure it out when she gets home."

Her eyes narrowed, jaw twisting to the side as if she were offended. "What are you doing out here anyway?" she asked, pressing her fist into her cocked hip.

I looked behind me, where the mop rested against the wall in the bucket. She'd tracked footprints across the still-wet porch.

"Just mopping. I think we may do some pictures up here, so I wanted to be sure the porch wasn't dirty or anything." I looked away from her, trying not to meet her eye.

"I thought you'd forgotten about the pictures?"

"Oh, right, well I…" I trailed off, unable to focus. Behind her head, I noticed a spatter of blood on the white, wooden column that connected the porch to the over-hanging roof.

"Everything okay, Peter?"

I darted my gaze back to her. "Yeah, why do you ask?"

"You seem…off."

"I'm fine."

"How are things between you two? I didn't get a chance to check in with you the other night."

I looked in the house, checking to make sure the kids weren't around. "Things are fine, Glennon."

"Have you told her?"

I groaned, locking my jaw as I looked back out into the yard. "I can't yet."

"You don't have a choice, Peter."

"I do. *We* do. We don't have to hurt her like this."

"She's going to find out sooner or later. Isn't it better if it comes from you than me?"

"We're going to break her heart, Glennon... How can that be what you want?"

She stepped sideways, moving until I was looking at her, and I focused on the dangling golden moon earring hanging from her earlobe.

"Of course it's not what I want. She's my best friend, Peter. I love her more than anything. But she deserves to know the truth. We owe her that much."

"I know," I said, kicking the porch with my heel. It was the truth, but that didn't make it sting any less badly. "I will tell her. I promised you I would. I just need time."

"I've given you time. But I'm not going to keep letting you off the hook. Tell her soon, or I will." She tucked a piece of her caramel-colored hair behind her ears.

I swallowed, looking down and squeezing my eyes shut. When I looked back up, I said, "I said okay, Glennon."

She tilted her head to the side, reaching out to touch my arm, but I jerked it back. "You should probably get going. I need to get the kids up and fed before she gets home."

Glennon laughed without missing a beat. "Yeah. Good luck with that."

"Thanks for the coffee."

"Anytime." She turned to walk away, but it was hesitant. I knew she didn't want to.

"Thanks for the offer, too," I called, feeling guilty for asking her to leave. I needed to keep things peaceful between us. She had the power to end my marriage, and if I didn't keep her happy, she just might. "About the pictures, I mean."

She spun back around, meeting my eye. There was a sadness there I hadn't expected. "Anytime on that, too. You know I'm always here for you guys."

"I know," I admitted, taking another sip of my coffee for good measure. "Give Seth my best, will ya?"

"Sure thing." She skipped off down the porch back to her SUV in a flash, and the second she was out of the driveway, I let out a loud, exhausted sigh of relief, blinking back sudden tears. I wasn't sure I'd ever be able to live with such fear. It was terrifying, every minute of every day, having all my secrets weighing down on me.

I reached for the mop, remembering the blood on the column beside Glennon's head. I was too afraid to leave the blood for even the amount of time it would take to get a cloth, so I lifted the mop into the air, wiping it away vigorously. Rust-colored water dripped down the white, wooden board, and I continued to wipe and dip, wipe and dip, until it was all cleaned.

Then, I looked around at the rest of the columns and

back at the door, realizing how much I'd managed to miss. Everywhere I looked, there were specks of blood. Evidence. Proof of the horrible crime I'd committed. I sighed, running a hand through my hair.

How was I ever going to make this okay again?

CHAPTER NINETEEN

AINSLEY

I approached the officers standing outside the branch the way you'd approach a deranged man with a gun. Every step was cautious as I tried to keep my face still, no sudden movements.

Brendan's and Tara's cars were in the parking lot, though they were nowhere to be seen. Noticing me approaching, two male officers ended their conversation, looking up at me.

"We're sorry, ma'am, you won't be able to enter the branch right now."

"I...I work here." I glanced toward the building, realizing the all-clear hadn't gone up yet. Where were Brendan and Tara? "I'm the manager. Did something happen?" Maybe the cops weren't there for me, after all.

"What's your name?" one of the officers asked, looking down at the pad of paper in his hands.

"Ainsley Greenburg," I told him. "Can you tell me what's going on?"

"There was a suspicious car here when your employees

arrived. A woman driving a red Hyundai Santa Fe. Your employees were afraid she may have been plotting to rob them. They called us to check it out, but the SUV had left by the time we arrived. We are getting a good look around the building to make sure it's safe for you all to enter."

"Where are my employees?" I asked, looking over toward their cars. "Why didn't they call me?"

As soon as I'd asked, I noticed the shape of a head inside Brendan's car. Tara's too. They were okay.

"They're waiting inside their cars until we give them the okay to get out. We'll have to ask you to do the same. The alarm wasn't set off, so once we've made sure the perimeter is secure, you'll be allowed to head inside. I think it was likely a case of someone parking here for a moment, maybe to answer a phone call or check their GPS, but we'd rather be safe than sorry. The employees did the right thing."

I supposed I must have looked angry, because he said the last sentence affirmatively, as if I needed to hear it. "Yes, of course. Thank you for coming."

"It's our job, ma'am."

"I...I appreciate that," I said softly, still trying to process everything I was being told.

"If you'll wait in your car, then." He gestured to the car, and I backed away from the officers, making my way back to the safety of my vehicle with a racing heart. Why hadn't they tried to call me? I glanced down at my phone, preparing to text them and noticed the missed call, one I hadn't seen come in as I was talking to Glennon. What if they'd been in real trouble? How had I let everything get so out of control? My branch and employees were my responsibility, and when they'd needed me most, I'd let them down. How could I have been so stupid?

I pressed my fingers into my temples.

Pull yourself together, Ainsley. You have to pull yourself together, or you're going to ruin everything.

WHEN I ARRIVED home that afternoon, Peter was on the porch on his hands and knees, scrubbing the exterior wall of the house with a dirty washcloth, a bucket of brown water beside him. The mop was lying in front of the door.

"What are you doing?"

"Cleaning," he said, not looking up at me. He seemed almost manic. The walls appeared fine to me, but he was insistent, so I didn't argue.

"Everything okay?"

"Fine," he snipped. "You know, you could've told me that you told Glennon we were doing family pictures. Prepared me a little so I wouldn't be caught off guard when she showed up here this morning to help."

My stomach flopped. "She did what?"

He stopped scrubbing. "You didn't know?"

"I had no idea. I told her not to come over. She wanted to spend time together, go for drinks or coffee or something, but I told her we were doing pictures to buy us time. I didn't expect her to come over." He looked at me, his lips pursed, as if that were ridiculous. "Did she stay long?"

"She caught me in the middle of cleaning. I told her we were fine and didn't need help, and she left."

"You weren't rude, were you?"

"Ainsley, I'm literally washing *blood*," he lowered his voice to a whisper as he said the last word, "off our walls. I think I have more important things to worry about than hurting your friend's feelings."

I groaned. "Whatever. I'll have to call her later and fix things. What did you tell her about pictures?"

"That I didn't need help. That you were picking out the outfits."

I nodded. "Fine. Do you need some help with this?"

He looked away from me, back to his work. "I'm almost done. Did you take care of the..."

"Yep, it's gone." I glanced around behind me, checking out the quiet drive to be sure no one was coming down it, feeling exposed, even in the privacy of our very secluded yard.

"I was thinking... Maybe tonight we can move the...*thing*—" He cleared his throat. "To the woods. Somewhere far away from the house." He gestured toward the thick, dark woods surrounding us. We only owned about three acres, but were enveloped by over forty acres of hunting ground owned by various people. There were plenty of places to hide a body, but it was risky. Too risky.

"Do you know how many hunting cameras are in these woods? What if we were caught?" I asked, watching as he continued to scrub the clean spot.

"Well, then we'll bury it in our portion. Where there are no cameras."

"If they come looking, that's the first place they'll check. And I don't want you digging the *thing* up. We have to leave it alone."

The body was no longer a he, but an it. We'd made that transition.

Were there five steps to processing the fact that you'd committed a murder like there were for grief?

Step 1. Cleaning up.

Step 2. Detaching yourself from the victim by refusing to acknowledge they existed.

Step 3. To be determined

"Besides that," I added, "returning to the scene of a crime is the worst thing we can do right now."

"Ainsley, we live at the scene of the crime. We can't just keep him there. I can handle it. I can find somewhere to put him—"

"I said no. You're going to get caugh—"

"Mom?" a faint voice interrupted my sentence, calling from inside the house, and I realized Maisy was standing in the living room, hair wild, one eye squeezed shut. She yawned, catching my eye through the glass of the door.

I opened it, putting on my best *everything's fine* smile. "Good morning, sleepy head."

"What are you doing?"

"Your dad's cleaning the porch. I just got home. Did you have fun last night? I didn't get a chance to talk to you very much after you got home."

"It was homework, so it wasn't fun." She laughed, then her eyes filled with concern. "Dylan said you were sick. Are you better now?"

"Much. I think I ate something off at dinner."

"Nicole's dad says there's a bad stomach bug going around right now. He said he's had sixteen different patients this week with it."

"I don't think that's what I had. I'm feeling so much better already," I assured her, pleased to see the worry disappear. "Anyway, why don't you go on into the kitchen and get yourself some lunch, okay? I'll be inside in a second."

"Okay," she said, rubbing her eyes as she released another yawn and sulked to the kitchen.

"Do you think she heard us?" Peter asked, filling me with brand-new concern.

I shook my head. "She couldn't have... Could she?"

"Had she been standing there long?" As he asked, he stood up, dropped the sponge in the bucket, and dusted his hands on his pants.

"I have no idea," I said, inhaling deeply through my nose. I couldn't think about it. I refused to. There was no way she'd heard, and even if she had, no way she'd understood what we were talking about. I stepped a foot inside the house, glancing back at him. "I'm going to change and fix myself some lunch. You should hurry up with this and join us." I met his eyes, my gaze stern. "And wipe that petrified look off your face."

CHAPTER TWENTY

PETER

The rest of the day went smoothly, or as smoothly as could be expected. Ainsley made grilled cheese sandwiches and chicken soup for lunch, a fall favorite comfort food she made whenever any of the kids were sick. I wasn't sure if she was doing it to help further the narrative that she'd been sick the day before, or because what we both needed more than anything, was comfort. Either way, I was grateful for it.

Things could go on. Normal things were still happening. I'd helped her load the dishwasher, despite the body buried under our porch. I'd played a video game with Riley, despite the way my fingers still burned from the over-exposure to bleach. I watched a sitcom with Maisy, despite my racing heart when the main couple hit a raccoon with their car and thought, for a split second, it had been a person. I'd helped fold and put away the laundry that had been splattered with blood the night before. I could be normal; I could do normal things.

I picked up a novel after the kids had gone to their

rooms, but my eyes glazed over the words. Refusing to put it down, I continued to stare at the words. At some point, I'd find a way to read them. All that mattered was that I was pulling it off. I could pretend to go through the motions, doing everything I needed to do, despite my mind being elsewhere. I was beginning to master it. Pretending to be a living, breathing person while I melted internally into an anxious mess.

Ainsley had been watching me all afternoon, her cool gaze meeting mine intently across the room. I'd feel a chill run over me, the distinct knowing that someone was watching, look up, and there she was. There was something eerie about her level of calm. It didn't sit right with me. Had she shut down after what had happened? Was she calmer because she wasn't the murderer? I didn't know, but I wished I did.

Ainsley picked up the remote from the arm of the couch, flipping through the channels. When I heard the voice of a familiar news anchor, I looked up. I'd purposefully been avoiding social media and the news, hoping not to hear anything that would make me feel so much worse. I'd rather not know.

It was my turn to stare at her, my brows furrowed as they went to the weatherman to hear about an incoming storm. After a few seconds, she blinked, looking in my direction, her face still and stony.

"We have to know," she said, reading my expression. "We have to be prepared."

"What if it's bad?"

"We deal with it," she said. "Together."

"But—" My phone buzzed beside me, interrupting my

argument and causing my skin to grow cold. Every time it had gone off all day, I'd panicked, sure the number on the screen would signal my demise. How could anyone get away with killing a cop? Each time, though, it had been a promotional email or social media notification.

I stared at the screen this time, a text message from Gina. It was the first I'd heard from her since the night before. I wondered how angry she must be with me. I couldn't blame her if she was, but the idea of arguing or trying to explain what had happened made me sick to my stomach.

I opened the text message.

"What is it?" Ainsley asked.

What happened last night? Just wanted to check in and make sure everything's okay.

I felt relieved, though pressured at the same time. How was I ever going to explain what happened? Or why I left? "It's Gina from work. Making sure everything's okay. I didn't explain why I had to rush out last night." I didn't look up as I said it, typing out my response.

Sorry I had to rush out. I'll pay you back for dinner. Family emergency...

Her response was almost instant: **I hope everything's okay? Anything I can do?**

No, but I appreciate the offer. I'll explain on Monday.

"What did you tell her?" she asked.

"Nothing. That we had a family emergency." I laid my phone facedown on the couch.

"You have to tell her I was sick. We have to keep our story straight across all channels."

I nodded. "Okay, I'll tell her that Monday. It's fine."

"Speaking of," she said, "after this, I need to call Glennon and smooth things over."

"What are you going to tell her about the pictures?"

"That the photographer got sick or something," she said. "I'll make something up."

"Photographer?" I asked, cocking my head to the side. "She said you told her we were using a tripod."

Ainsley turned to look at me, her face ashen. "What?"

"She said you said we were—"

"No. I told her you'd hired your coworker's daughter."

I swallowed. "No, I'm sure that's not what she told me. Maybe you were—"

"I know what I said," she said, shaking her head as she stood from the couch. "Glennon was testing you... She wanted to prove I was lying."

"Well, how was I supposed to know that?" I demanded.

The sigh that escaped her throat said I'd done something awful, but I had no idea why it was the end of the world. Not compared to everything else we had going on. "Call her and explain. It'll be fine."

"How would you like me to explain?" she asked, pressing her lips together as she stared at me, phone in hand. "I can't tell her the truth."

"Just tell her I didn't know what I was talking about."

"It was *your* coworker's daughter who was supposed to be our photographer, Peter. You would've been the one to hire her."

"Then...tell her we were having family night."

"Glennon and Seth come to half our family nights." She put air quotes around the words *family night*. "Why wouldn't I have invited them if that were the case?" She shook her head, rubbing her temple and walking across the room. "I have to fix this."

"I'm sorry," I called after her, but she was already out of the room.

I stared back at the television, feeling like a child who'd been scolded and sent to his room. The news anchors were discussing a local food and toy drive for the upcoming holiday. I lowered the volume, hoping to hear what Ainsley was telling Glennon.

"I have a confession..." I heard her say in a low voice. "The other night, when you asked if Peter and I are having problems, I wasn't being honest with you."

There was a pause.

"Yeah, I mean, we are, but it's worse than I let on. They aren't huge, don't worry... We're...you know, we're hanging in there, but it's not great."

I felt the sting of her words. Was that how she felt, or was she lying again? She was only trying to smooth things over with Glennon, wasn't she?

"Anyway, that's why I lied to you today. We were planning a stay-in date night sort of thing, and it was too embarrassing to admit."

She paused again.

"No, I know that. I do tell you everything. Almost everything. I don't know why this was so hard... I thought about asking you to watch the kids, but they're all off in their own worlds these days, it's not like they were a bother." She paused again, and then there was a laugh. I felt my muscles relax immediately.

"Yeah, he's been doing all sorts of chores around here

lately. I've been complaining about that porch for months. At least he's trying... Oh, yes. That sounds great. We'll plan for dinner tomorrow, then... Okay. See you then. Yep, love you too."

There was silence in the kitchen, no sounds of footsteps or movement at all, then I heard her shuffling across the floor. When she reappeared in the living room, she smiled stiffly at me.

"Glennon and Seth want us to come over tomorrow for dinner."

"Now isn't a good time, Ainsley..."

"Why not?" she asked, her eyes wide and purposefully innocent. After a moment of me trying to decide a response, she said, "We have to keep everything up as normal. We have to keep living our lives, Peter."

The dead cop under our porch doesn't get to keep living his life. "Did you have to tell her we were having problems?"

"I had to fix the lie. It was the only way."

I didn't tell her I could've come up with a hundred other solutions that didn't involve marital issues, but it wasn't as if Glennon didn't know we'd had issues in the past. "Fine. Whatever. What time tomorrow?"

"Sev—" She started to answer but stopped, turning her attention to the television screen, her jaw agape. "Turn it up..." came the horrified whisper.

I followed her gaze to where a blonde news anchor sat at a desk. In the corner of the screen, a small photo of a bald-headed, sharp-featured man in a cop's uniform was placed. The ticker across the screen read **Police ask for help in search for missing officer.**

I turned up the volume, listening closely as the anchor began to speak.

"Police today are reporting that a local law enforcement officer has gone missing. Stefan De Luca, forty-six, a decorated Army veteran and member of the Arrington police force for nearly twenty years, was reported missing when he did not report for his shift this morning at eight a.m. Officer De Luca's fellow officers say it is unheard of for him to not report for a shift, and they have been unable to reach him all day. De Luca's wife, Illiana De Luca, was on a business trip in Oakland, California, at the time that her husband disappeared, but she is home now and asking for the public's help to locate her missing husband. We'll talk to her when we come back."

The screen filled with a red and white transition, breaking away to a car commercial, and I looked over at my wife, who, for the first time all day, looked utterly terrified.

I felt as though I were going to be sick as I stared at her, a bitter taste forming in my mouth. *"He had a wife?"*

CHAPTER TWENTY-ONE

AINSLEY

We'd left the kids at home alone with clear instructions not to leave the house or answer the door as we headed to Seth and Glennon's, not much room for talking in the thick silence that filled the car. When we pulled into their driveway, I'd picked the nail polish off most of my fingernails.

"Ready?" Peter asked, switching off the car. He was pale, his hands still gripped tightly to the wheel.

"It's going to be fine," I assured him, though I didn't feel that way at all. "Act normal. We have to pretend everything's normal."

He opened his car door without another word and walked around the front of it to meet me at the edge of their yard. We walked across the dying grass, littered with red and yellow leaves, to reach their front porch. As soon as we stepped foot on it, the front door swung open and Seth appeared.

His crooked smile filled his stubble-coated face. He ran a hand over his dark, buzzed hair and stepped back to hold the door open. "'Bout time you two showed up," he joked, hugging me before shaking Peter's hand.

Peter gave a low laugh, pulling him in for a one-armed hug. "How's work?" he asked as he released him. Under normal circumstances, I'd walk away from them as their conversation faded into shop talk, but that night, I didn't want to leave Peter alone. I was too worried he'd panic and say or do something incriminating.

Seth and Glennon were our best friends, but did I believe they would cover up something like this? And even if they did, did I believe they'd still look at us the same? The truth was that I couldn't expect them to look at us the same when *I* couldn't even look at us the same.

"Work's good," Seth said, sighing. "We had this killer merger in Toronto, so we've been dealing with trying to keep everything running smoothly..." I watched Peter wince at his use of the word *killer*, though Seth didn't seem to notice. "Always a pain in the ass, but the acquisition will be worth it in the long run. What about you? How're things? How's business? How're the kids?"

Peter was nodding excessively, not responding, a thin sheen of sweat on his brow. I put a hand on his arm. "The kids are well," I said. "And Peter got asked to weigh in on the redevelopment downtown." Peter met my eye, a small smile on his lips, then he looked back at Seth, seeming to regain his footing.

Seth gasped. "Is that right? That could be huge!"

Falling into a rhythm, Peter's shoulders seemed to relax as he said, "Yeah, it's looking great. It'll be nice to know I had a hand in making the skyline what it'll be. I've got the few buildings downtown right now, but this'll be...it'll be the biggest deal of my career thus far. "

"That's excellent, man. Hey, you want a beer?" Seth pointed down the hall, toward the den that had been converted to a man cave.

Without looking my way again, Peter nodded. "You bet."

"Want us to grab you anything, Ainsley?" Seth asked, pointing a finger gun in my direction.

"Nope, I'll grab some wine with Glennon. You boys have fun."

Seth tossed an arm around Peter's shoulders as they walked away. "Okay, so you'll never believe what happened... Canada, man, it's wild..."

I turned away from them, heading for the kitchen where Glennon had a spread of food laid out.

"Mmm, something smells good," I said, startling her. She turned around, a wide grin on her face.

"I thought I heard you come in. Sorry, I was just trying to get this finished up."

"No worries." I hugged her close, kissing her cheek briefly before moving toward the half-empty bottle of wine on the counter. "What are we having?"

"We're trying something new tonight."

"That's brave," I said, pulling a glass down from the cabinet.

"It's called cauliflower tacos with cashew crema," she said, donning an accent, though I wasn't sure where it was supposed to be from.

"That sounds...interesting," I said, taking a sip of the wine and grabbing a carrot from the veggie tray. I dipped it in hummus before popping it into my mouth. The food looked delicious. The cauliflower that filled the shell was browned, covered in dashes of cilantro and onion.

"We're going vegan," she announced. "I watched this documentary on Netflix, and I swear I'll never eat meat again."

"Of course you did." I nodded. Glennon was always looking for the next new thing, be it a diet, activity, or career.

"Hold me to it; you have to swear. It's disgusting what they do to these poor animals. I'm making you watch it with me again."

"Sounds delightful. I'm looking forward to it," I teased. "And how's the diet going so far?"

"It's not a diet, love." She put her hands out, held in Jnana Mudra as if she were meditating. "It's a lifestyle."

"Well, how's your lifestyle going, then?" I asked, eating another carrot with a smirk on my face.

"We started yesterday, and I've stuck with it," she said proudly. "Even Seth is going along with this one. His cholesterol has been up at the last few doctor's appointments."

"Good for you, babe," I said seriously. "I'm proud of you. This is one diet I can get on board with. And you know I'll eat anything you make. I don't think you've ever made anything I don't like."

She laughed, loud and boisterous, and picked up her glass of wine. "Have you forgotten about the cookies I made with almond flour when we were on keto?"

I laughed with her, remembering it well. *The sand cookies!* Oh my god, how did I forget? Okay, fair enough, I take it back. *Most* of the things you cook are delicious, so I'm sure these will be, too."

"I've got beans and rice as a side, so if we don't like these, we have a backup. And veggies, lots and lots of veggies."

"Lovely. Let me help you carry them to the table." I reached for the jars of sauce sitting on the counter, and she touched my arm, stopping me from walking away. When I looked over at her, her face was serious.

"Hey, before the guys get back in here... What happened?" she asked, keeping her voice barely above a whisper. "Are you guys okay?"

I forced a smile. "Oh, yeah. It's okay, it's nothing."

"Did he do something wrong?"

I shook my head, my lips pressed together. "Not really, no."

She appeared hurt, releasing my arm. "Why are you shutting me out so much lately? Have I done something wrong?"

"No!" I said. "Of course not. No, it's an issue with Peter and me, and he feels uncomfortable with me talking too much about it. You know I'll tell you everything when I can."

"Is he cheating on you?"

My breathing quickened, and I forced myself to look away. "Why would you ask that?"

"Because he's a man," she said flatly.

I shook my head, moving into the dining room. "It's nothing like that, trust me. You know I wouldn't be sticking around if that was it."

She stopped in her tracks, and when I reached the

table and looked back in her direction, she seemed hurt. Before I could say anything, she asked, "You'd leave him?"

"Of course I would." I scoffed. "Was there ever any question?"

"Just like that? You wouldn't consider counseling or...I mean, what about the kids?"

I cocked my head to the side, placing the jars onto the table. "Is there any amount of counseling that would make a cheater less of a cheater? And as for the kids, I wouldn't want any of them to stay in a loveless marriage, so why would I stay in one myself?"

"But...just because he cheated...it doesn't mean he doesn't love you."

"What are you talking about, Glennon?" I asked her, hearing the men's voices growing near the room. "Where is this coming from?"

"Nothing. You know me. I'm just rambling," she said, her face growing red as she shuffled past me and set the platter of food down. Moments later, our husbands reappeared, beers in hand, and joined us at the table. Glennon wouldn't meet my eyes as we sat, and Seth filled the silence with talk of his travels and the merger.

I wasn't listening, only nodding along as I ran her question over and over in my head.

What was she talking about?

Why had she asked so many questions about Peter cheating on me?

What did she know?

CHAPTER TWENTY-TWO

PETER

Ainsley was strangely quiet at dinner. I kept trying to draw her attention to me, to find an explanation for her silence, but she was giving me nothing. She'd hardly looked my way at all, and even when she did, she was distant, her eyes foggy and lost.

When dinner was over, she excused herself to go to the restroom, her voice shaky and soft. Something had happened.

Seth looked at me, then Glennon.

"Is...everything okay?"

Glennon's jaw tightened. "I don't think she's feeling all that well."

I stood from the table, taking my cue. "I should go talk to her," I said, hurrying from the room as rapidly as I could without looking insane. I made my way down the hall before I heard footsteps coming from behind me.

"Peter." I turned around, shocked to see Glennon coming up behind me.

"Yeah?"

She nodded her head toward their guest bedroom to our left. "We should talk."

I swallowed. Those words never preceded good news, and I wasn't in the mood to be berated by Glennon's moral compass about what I should or shouldn't tell my wife and when.

"Okay..." I followed her into the bedroom, and she shut the door, flicking on the light.

I'd been in the room a few times before, even spent the night there once or twice. It was familiar, the walls a bright, light yellow. The bed in the center of the room had a wrought iron frame with a matching floral yellow and navy blue comforter and throw pillows. It was the only room in the house that still had carpet, though from what Seth had told me, they were planning to tear it up next summer.

Outside, the world was dark, and inside the sterile, too-bright room, everything was still.

"What's up?" I asked, clearing my throat.

Glennon narrowed her gaze at me. "Don't 'what's up' me. Why haven't you told her?"

My blood went cold as I studied her expression. Was that why Ainsley was so upset? Had Glennon told her about us?

"I haven't had a chance. We've had a lot going on, Glennon. You don't know the half of it."

"I know there's always an excuse with you. Between the kids, the house, work, school... You've always got a reason not to tell her. You need to rip off the Band-Aid."

"Did you say something to her?" I demanded, pointing my finger toward the door.

"Of course, I didn't. I promised I'd give you the chance to do it. We agreed it should come from you."

"I know we did, and I'm going to tell her. You need to back off."

"Don't," she said, her voice sharp and pained. "Don't you dare tell me to back off. I could tell her right now, Peter. I could tell her the truth and end your marriage before you even walk out of here. But that's not what I want. Not for Ainsley...or you either."

"What do you want, then, Glennon? What is it that you want? And you still haven't told Seth anything, have you? Why am I the one who has to break the news first?"

"Do you think, for one second, that as soon as I tell Seth, he's not going to come after you? And then Ainsley's sure to find out. I'm letting you tell her out of respect for her. Because I'd rather her find out in a way that she can process it all before all of our worlds implode."

"It doesn't have to be this way. We don't have to tell them anything. We can pretend it never happened," I said, a sinking feeling growing in the pit of my stomach.

"I can't do that to her. I can't look at her every single day and know I'm holding in this lie. I can't face Seth every day and pretend everything's fine. Ainsley has to know the truth. I can't keep doing this. If she finds out I've kept this from her all this time... Oh, who am I kidding? She's going to hate me no matter what." She sighed, shaking her head. "I hate this, Peter. I do. I don't know what to do. You have to tell her."

"Please, Glennon. You don't understand—"

"Either you tell her, or I will."

"Look, now is not the time. I know I've said that to you

a million times, but if there were ever a *not the time*, this is it."

"I don't care anymore, Peter. I don't care about getting on your schedule. She deserves to know."

"I agree, trust me. I've been trying to tell her. We're working on us, getting better. But you can't do this right now. Please, Glennon, I'm begging you. You need to give me more time to sort things out."

"You can sort all you'd like, *after* you tell my best friend the truth..." She crossed her arms. "I'm giving you the week, and then I'm telling her. A week, do you hear me? No extensions this time, Peter. If you want me to be there, to help explain, I will. But she needs to know the truth, and I'm done waiting."

"I'm sorry, Glennon. I'm so, so sorry."

"I appreciate the apology, but you don't owe it to me. And, if you do, you owe her one more. We both do. So help me God, Peter, you'd better figure out what or who it is that you want and figure it out soon. Before you lose everything."

The door to the bathroom opened, and I heard Ainsley's quiet footsteps padding down the hall. We remained still and silent, listening to her get farther away. Once she was past, Glennon put her hand on the doorknob.

"She told me she'd leave you if you ever cheated. I don't know if that's what you want..."

"*No*," I said, shaking my head. "Of course not. I love her, Glennon."

"Then tell her the truth and let the cards fall where they may." She jerked open the door and sauntered out, flicking the light out as she disappeared from the room.

CHAPTER TWENTY-THREE

AINSLEY

"Someone's here to see you."

I peeked my head around my desk, searching through the glass that separated me from the lobby, looking for a familiar customer. To my surprise, there was only one person waiting in the lobby, a woman with a wavy, black bob and steely eyes.

"Did she say what she needs?"

"She didn't. She asked if you worked here..."

I inhaled sharply then composed myself. "Thank you, Tara." Placing the phone down, I stood from behind my desk and stepped out into the lobby, my hands clasped together in front of me. My heels clicked across the lobby without caution, the smile on my face showing warmth and peace. I'd always been able to control the way I came across to people, even when I was the complete opposite internally.

"Hi," I said, extending my hand toward her. "I'm Ainsley Greenburg. How can I help you today?"

She made no attempt to smile. Instead, she stood from

the stiff couch in the center of our lobby, returning the hand shake and clearing her throat.

"My name's Illiana De Luca. Perhaps we should go inside your office."

I nodded, my throat too dry at the sound of her name. Was it a coincidence?

"Of course," I squeaked. I turned, gesturing that she should lead the way. Once we were inside my office, away from prying ears, she sat down across from me, clasping her hands together in her lap. *Breathe, Ainsley.* "Now, was there something I could do for you?"

"There is, actually. I was hoping you might be able to tell me where my husband is."

A chill swept over me at her words, and I stared at her brown, sorrow-filled eyes, making sense of their cool quality. I remembered her name from the news, but I didn't want to believe it.

Keep it together. You have no idea who her husband is.

"Your husband? Does he have an account with us?"

She shook her head, pressing her lips into a thin line. "Don't patronize me, Ainsley. I know you were sleeping with Stefan. Do you know where he is? Why he isn't returning my calls? Why he hasn't shown up for work in three days?"

I tried to collect myself while refusing to break eye contact. I wouldn't let her see the lie in my expression. "I'm so sorry... I don't know where he is. We weren't sleeping together. I had no idea he was married, but we only went out on one date. We didn't even kiss."

The woman's tone grew more frustrated. "I don't care about any of that. Stefan and I had a complicated marriage. I know he went to visit you on the night he disappeared."

My whole body tensed, fear palpable in the room. I wondered if she could feel it, too. "If he did, he either never made it to me or he missed me. I only saw him one time..." I paused, chewing my bottom lip. "Does he have family? Friends? Maybe he went out of town?"

"That wouldn't explain him not answering my calls," she snipped.

"I'm so sorry. I didn't know him well, but I hope he is found safe. He was...very kind to me." I looked down for the first time, forcing away thoughts of his kindness on our first date. "Again, I'm so sorry about the circumstances. I had no idea about you. I'd never..." I shook my head. "I didn't want anyone to get hurt—you included."

Suddenly, I was thinking about what we'd done. What we'd taken from her. What would I do if someone took Peter from me? If the woman he'd dated had caused his death? My lips pressed together until it was painful, and I released them.

"I doubt that," she said, not bothering to try and hide her disgust with me. "You're married, too, aren't you?"

"H-how could you know that?" Realization swept over me. "I'm sorry, how did you even know about me? How did you find me?"

"My husband was a cop, Mrs. Greenburg. Do you think we didn't look into the women he was seeing? Made sure they seemed normal? Sane?" She studied my expression. "I know all about you."

"I'm sorry, *women?* Plural? He was seeing multiple people? And you knew about it?"

"The intricacies of my marriage are none of your concern—"

"Of course not, I would never, I—"

"But what should be your concern is the fact that I'm going to tell the detectives working his case all about you. I'm going to tell them where you live, your children's names, your husband's name. We're going to get to the bottom of this. I wanted to give you a chance to come clean, to tell me the truth without involving the law. If you know where he is and you're hiding it from me, or if you've done something wrong and you're lying, we'll figure it out. But not before your life, your children's lives, are dragged through the hassles of a criminal investigation."

There was no doubt in her eyes, no sign that she was bluffing. She was going to make sure the truth was found out. She was going to make sure I went down for it.

"Are you sure you don't have anything you want to tell me?" she asked, reaching for the brown, oversized handbag she'd placed in the seat next to her.

"I'm sorry, I have no idea..." I whispered half-heartedly.

She sighed, standing up. "Well, if you think of anything, you should be sure to tell Detective Chad." She pulled a card from the bag and laid it down in front of me. "I'm going to give him your contact information tonight." She turned, grabbing hold of the doorknob without another word.

"Wait," I cried, standing up. She spun back around, a knowing look in her eyes. "I can't talk here... I don't know a lot, but I might know something. I'll tell you everything

I know, but I can't do it here. This is my place of business. I have customers waiting."

"My husband is missing," she argued. "I hardly care about overdraft fees."

"I understand. I want to help. Please, just... Please. Come to my house this evening. We can talk alone. Me and you. We can discuss everything." She hesitated, watching me closely with a dubious expression. "I know you don't know me that well, and I don't know him that well, but he seems very sweet. I want you to find him."

She nodded slowly, wary of the offer. "Fine. What time do you get off?"

"Five. I can meet you at my house at six."

"Fine," she repeated.

"My address is—"

"I know." Without allowing me to finish, she pulled the door open and marched out. "I'll see you at six."

As I watched her disappear from the lobby, a sharp, ragged breath escaped my lungs, and I clutched my chest. I hurried over to the door, watching her climb into a red Hyundai Santa Fe and realized it matched the description of the car my employees had seen outside the branch Saturday morning.

How long had Illiana De Luca been looking for me?

And what was she planning to do now that she'd found me?

CHAPTER TWENTY-FOUR

PETER

My job was to get the kids out of the house while Ainsley attempted to talk to the woman who wanted to ruin our lives. Sounds simple enough, right?

My wife wanted to talk to her, to explain a few things. I thought it was dangerous, thought it was reckless to bring someone into our world, to tell her Ainsley had known her husband at all.

Ainsley said we had no choice.

Getting the kids to go to friends' houses was no problem; they were always excited to get out of the house, so my only responsibility was dropping them each off at their respective locations.

Ainsley had told me to stay away from the house, but I couldn't. I needed to be there. To protect her. To help her in case she got stuck in a lie. So, when I walked back through the front door only forty-five minutes after I'd left, I was met by two icy glares.

"I'm so sorry," Ainsley said, standing up and gesturing

toward me. "This is my husband, Peter. Peter, this is Illiana De Luca."

"It's nice to meet you," I said, extending a hand. She stared at it oddly but made no move to return the gesture.

"Honey, could you give us a few minutes? Maybe go work outside so we can talk?" Ainsley nodded encouragingly at me, making me feel like a child being sent outside to play.

I turned back around, though I was hardly prepared to work outside, still dressed in my work clothes. I walked out into the yard, refusing to look in the direction of the porch or the secret hidden beneath it.

I needed to get inside. I needed to be sure she was protecting me, but how? She'd all but locked me out of the house. I made my way around toward the back of the house as a new idea struck me. I pulled open the back screen door, wincing as its hinges let out a loud squeak. I was hopeful that it was far enough away from the living room that they wouldn't hear it, but I paused, listening for approaching footsteps anyway. I waited, half expecting my wife to appear and tell me to buzz off. When she didn't, I opened the door fully, sliding inside and shutting it behind me. I moved across the laundry room with silent footsteps.

Once in the hall, I could hear their hushed voices. I moved closer and closer toward them until, halfway down the hall, I could make out what they were saying.

"In the end, I couldn't go through with it," Ainsley said. "I love my husband very much. It was a mistake, and I told Stefan that much. He was kind to me that night. He said he understood. I'm seeing now that he understood my struggle more than I realized at the time, being married and all." I pressed myself against the wall, listening.

"He contacted me a few times after that, checking in to see how I was. I appreciated him. But then, the messages seemed almost obsessive." I heard her shudder and knew it was an act. But she was convincing to anyone who didn't know her as well as I did. "I stopped responding to him. I had no idea he was a police officer, but he'd started to scare me. I have no experience with online dating, so I was worried about what I'd gotten myself into."

"Stefan has a bit of an obsessive personality," Illiana admitted. "But he's harmless."

"I did lie to you before, though. Stefan did come to my house that night. It was out of the blue, and he seemed like he'd been drinking…" She paused, I assumed waiting to see if Illiana would say anything, but when she didn't, Ainsley continued, "I didn't let him in. After a few minutes of knocking, he left. I haven't heard from him since."

"But why did you lie when I asked you?"

"I'm sorry about that. I think more than anything, I was worried. I'm worried for Stefan, worried about my husband discovering my infidelity. But I wanted to tell you the truth, and if it helps you find him, then it's worth it to me."

"What time do you think he was here?" Illiana asked, all business.

"It was around seven thirty, maybe. I can't remember for sure."

"And your husband, what did he think was happening? Did he see him?"

"Thankfully, my husband was working late that evening. He came home shortly after Stefan left, but they missed each other. He doesn't know anything about him... I'd appreciate it if we could keep it that way."

I closed my hands into fists, feeling immense appreciation for my wife at that moment. If we made it through this, I was going to be better. I was going to be who she deserved. I swore it right then and there.

"I understand, but...I need you to come down to the police station with me. You can tell your husband whatever you'd like, but you have to tell the detectives what you've told me."

"I can't," Ainsley argued. "Peter would ask too many questions. Besides, like I told you, I don't know anything. If Stefan tries to contact me, I will let you know. You can leave your number with me, and—"

"No. No, that's not enough. For all we know, you were the last person to see my husband before he disappeared. Perhaps the last person to see him alive." Her words hung heavy in the air, and I heard Ainsley take a deep breath.

"He isn't dead," Ainsley said softly. "You shouldn't talk like that. He can't be dead."

"What other explanation is there? My husband loved his job, we had a happy marriage, I let him see other women when he wanted to. He was finishing up a few projects around the house. Last week, he'd booked us a vacation for next spring. He wasn't planning to leave me, Mrs. Greenburg. I know that much. Which means something bad has happened to him. You have to tell the police what you know."

I heard the fabric of the couch shift as someone stood.

Then, Ainsley said, "I can't, I told you. I had nothing to do with any of this."

"That's fine. I believe you, but you need to tell your story to the police. It could help."

"I'm not going with you. I'm sorry your husband is missing, but I have a family to take care of. I can't go running off to help you solve the mystery—"

"You can, and you will." My wife had met her match. I listened with a racing heart as the women bickered back and forth. "You have a responsibility to—"

"To what? To tell the police that I don't know anything about what happened to him? Surely you can manage that."

"How can you say that? How can you be so heartless? Surely you care that he's missing...that he's probably dead."

"You seem awfully certain of that for someone who's claiming to be innocent."

I heard the sharp inhale of the woman who wasn't my wife. "Excuse me? What is *that* supposed to mean?"

"Exactly what I said. How do I know you didn't do anything to him? Hm? For all I know, you were jealous of his affairs and decided to put an end to it, and now you're looking for someone to pin it all on. Maybe you don't want him found at all."

"How can you say that?" she asked, choking back tears. "I love my husband more than life. I've put up with everything because he means the world to me. I could never... would never...I didn't—"

A sharp, shrill ringing interrupted her and, for a moment, the room was still.

"Hello?"

Silence. I felt cool sweat gathering at my temples. "You what?" I took a step closer to the living room, stepping on a creaky spot on the floor. I froze, taking a half-step back as I tried to come up with my excuse. *I needed to go to the bathroom. I needed a drink of water. I was coming to change clothes.* "Are you sure?" Her voice interrupted my thoughts. "Yes. Okay. Sure, I'll be right down. Okay, thank you… Bye." The last word was whispered, breathless.

"What is it? Are you okay?" Ainsley asked, genuine concern in her voice as pure panic swelled in my stomach.

After a moment, Illiana said the words that shook me to my core, "No. I-I, um…I have to go. They…the police, they found his truck. They found Stefan's truck."

CHAPTER TWENTY-FIVE

AINSLEY

After Illiana left, I turned toward the doorway that led into the hall, where I knew Peter would be waiting. When he stepped out into the living room, it was of absolutely no shock to me. His face was ashen, his expression filled with panic.

"They found the truck?"

I nodded. "Don't panic. We knew this would happen."

"But already?" he asked. "And why is she here? Why would you bring her back to the house?"

"I needed to think, Peter. She freaked me out. I was caught off guard. I needed to collect myself, and this was the first thing I thought of. I thought bringing her here would help her see that we're a normal, *non-murdering* family."

"Except that we're not, Ains. And you brought her here, told her Stefan was here that night. What do you think is going to happen once she gets the police involved? If they get a warrant to search the property—"

"That isn't going to happen," she said, holding a hand

up to stop my rambling. "We're fine, Peter. Everything's fine. They don't have a body. They don't have any true reason to suspect us."

"What if they find your DNA in his car?"

"They won't," I said, his worried expression haunting. "I wore my hair up, with my hood over it. I wore gloves, a face mask. There should be no DNA there. And, even if there is, I didn't lie about going on a date with him. I can say we were in his car for a while."

"Were you?" he demanded.

I rolled my eyes. "That's hardly the concern right now, don't you think?"

"We can't let her tell them about you. About us. The last thing we need is for the police to be snooping around while we're still trying to get our story in order."

"What would you have me do, Peter? *Kill her?*"

He flinched at my words. "No. Of course not."

"Listen to me," I said calmly. "We have our story straight. He came over because I'd been ignoring him. I have the messages to prove that. I didn't answer the door. I called you to come home, but he'd left before you got here. That's all we know. We haven't heard from him since."

"That story gives me all the motive in the world."

"It doesn't. Not when the cheating was mutually agreed upon. You were seeing other people, too."

"I don't want that to come out. I don't want the police to know about it."

"Which is why I told Illiana I was cheating on you, but if it comes down to it, we'll tell them the truth."

"Aren't you the one who said we need to keep our story straight?"

"With the police, yes. But our marital issues aren't Illiana's concern, and that's what I'll tell the cops."

"I don't want this to get out," he said. "What will the kids think?"

"I hope it doesn't come to that, too," I agreed. "But right now, we have to wait and see what's going to happen."

"She's not going to give up."

"There's nothing for them to find," I said assertively. "We have to remain calm." I drew out the last two words. "That means you."

"I am calm," he said, though we both knew he was lying. "I think we need to move him."

"We can't do that," I snapped. "It's too risky."

"More risky than leaving him *buried under our porch?*" he asked, his cheeks growing splotchy with scarlet as his anger took over.

I stood my ground, my arms folded across my chest. "More risky than *un*burying him and trying to move him without getting caught."

He groaned. "I disagree. Having him here is the biggest risk, Ains. We have to be smart about this.

"I agree. And moving him would not be smart."

"I think it would," he said through gritted teeth.

"Well, I guess we'll have to agree to disagree, won't we?"

"But do what you decide anyway…"

I didn't nod, but I didn't need to. We both knew it was

how it would go. I was the only one who could think rationally in a moment of pressure.

It was why Peter had always been so impulsive in heated situations. While, under normal circumstances, he was prone to thinking things through thoroughly, in moments of fear or anger, he'd been known to lose control of himself. He let his fear, his passion, his worry, and his desire make decisions before his brain could.

He lived inside his head, where horrible outcomes were always right around the corner, and that quite often brought him to moments like this. Moments when he said or did the wrong thing and couldn't manage to stop it. No, if anyone was going to handle this, it would be me.

"I could go out there and do it anyway."

I scoffed, pinching the bridge of my nose in frustration. "Be my guest, Peter. That sounds like the smartest possible thing right now when we're sure our friend, Illiana, could be back any moment with the police. But sure, you go right ahead and get to digging."

Panic and anger swelled in me, each fighting to supersede the other. My vision began to tunnel at the thought of police pulling into the driveway. Police asking me to replay my version of events for them. Handcuffs on his wrists. The slam of prison bars.

"I need some air," he said, bringing me back to him.

"Where are you going?" I demanded, but he was past me before the sentence ended. He grabbed his coat from the rack by the door and stormed out of the house. I watched as he went but made no move to stop him. I needed space as much as he did.

CHAPTER TWENTY-SIX

PETER

I needed to stop thinking for a second. The decision I made next wasn't smart, but I wasn't entirely coherent. My usually clear thoughts were a foggy mess of worry, anger, rage, fear, exhaustion, and confusion. I needed clarity, and I tried to think of the last time I had true clarity.

That was how I found myself on Mallory's doorstep that evening, praying she was at home. I half expected her to ignore me when she came to the door, or worse yet, not remember me, but I had to try, and I couldn't chance reaching out to her on the app anymore.

I rapped my knuckles on the wood of the door, trembling with a mixture of excitement and nerves. I had no business being there. I wasn't oblivious to that fact. I just needed to feel something that wasn't worry for a few minutes, and being around Ainsley only made me feel more worried. More anxious. More—

"Gina?"

Gina stood in front of me wearing a black sports bra

and yoga pants. Her hair was tied in a messy bun on top of her head, with sweat collecting around the edges of her temples. She furrowed her brow, looking at the Apple Watch on her wrist and back at me. I stepped off the stoop, looking at the house number and back at my car.

"What are you doing here?" we asked at the same time.

"I'm sorry, what are you doing here?" I repeated.

"*I live here.* What are you doing here?" she asked.

Before I could piece together what was happening, Mallory descended the stairs and appeared behind her, wearing lounge pants and a floral tank top. As soon as she saw me, a bright smile lit up her face.

"Hey you," she called. "What are you doing here?"

Gina spun around, staring at Mallory and jutting her thumb in my direction. "You know him?"

"Of course, I know him. Why else would he be here? Let him in, would you?" Mallory's smile faded. "Wait a second, *you* know him?"

"Can someone please tell me what the hell is going on?" I asked, coming across angrier than I'd meant to. At that point, it felt like the universe was playing one giant prank on me.

"Pete's my date," Mallory said. "From the other night."

Gina looked back at me, her brows raised. "Oh, he is, is he?"

"How do you know him?" Mallory was looking at me as she asked.

"We work together," she explained, crossing her arms. I recognized that look. It was the one I'd seen her give in meetings when things weren't going our way. It was hard to piss Gina off, but once you had, things got ugly fast.

"Mallory and I just met," I told her, trying to decide which one I needed to justify knowing.

"You were the one she had sneaking out of here the other night," she said. It wasn't a question.

"I had no idea you lived here. If I had, I would've never…" I trailed off, unsure how to finish that sentence.

"You don't owe me an explanation," she snipped.

"Okay, now I think I'm the one who needs someone to explain to me what's going on…" Mallory said. "What am I missing?"

"Nothing's going on," Gina said, shaking her head, her lips pressed into a thin line. "Absolutely nothing." She backed away before I could say anything—not that I was sure *what* I should say—and disappeared down the hall.

Mallory watched her go with wide eyes then looked back at me. "Sorry, did you two have a thing or something? She seems pissed."

"Not exactly." I sighed. "I'm-I'm sorry. I should go talk to her."

"Excuse me?"

I walked past her, knocking on the door I'd watched Gina disappear into. She opened it immediately, standing before me with a grim expression. "You don't have to explain, Peter. Truly, you don't. You don't owe me anything."

"But I want to, okay?" I said. "I care about you. I don't want you to get the wrong impression."

"I just…I can't. I don't have time for this. I didn't want messy or complicated. That was the whole point. That's what we talked about."

"I'm not trying to make things complicated for you."

"You're sleeping with my roommate," she said, her voice echoing down the hall. I heard Mallory walk out of the townhome, slamming the front door. Her eyes followed her then landed back on me.

"I slept with her once," I said. "Yes. You're right."

"And I'm guessing you came back today to do the same thing."

"I just..." I felt vulnerability creeping in. "I needed someone to talk to. Someone who wouldn't judge me."

"Is that what you want, Peter? To talk?"

I nodded as she tapped her fingers against the wood of the door, contemplating. She sighed and stepped back. "Come in."

I walked into her bedroom, shocked and relieved to see that it was triple the size of Mallory's and starkly opposite in hygiene. There were no plates of rotting food or piles of clothing lying around. Instead, the room was pristine. Her closet was neat and color coordinated, her bed made, desk with a laptop in the corner tidy and organized. To my surprise, I realized the room smelled like her. I hadn't realized I knew her scent until that moment, but being in that space, I was brought back to the office and the many times she'd leaned over to hand me a stack of papers or come near me to point to a place where I'd need to sign. It was warm and sweet, filling me with a strange sense of calm.

"Thank you," I said as she shut the door. She crossed her arms, staring at me as she waited for me to start saying whatever it was I needed to say. "First of all, I wanted to apologize again for ditching you in the middle of dinner the other night."

She didn't respond.

"Like I told you, there was an emergency at home, and I didn't have a choice... I had to rush. I was hoping to see you at work today so I could pay you back for the meals and explain better."

"I called out," she said. "Not because of you. I needed some time for myself."

"Sure... I totally understand," I said eagerly, pulling out my wallet. "How much was it? I want to cover both our meals."

She reached out, putting her hand over my wallet and pushing it away. "I don't want your money, Peter. I make practically the same salary as you, and I don't have a family to support. Trust me, I've got it."

"Well, I'd still like to pay."

"I don't want it," she said.

I felt myself growing warm with embarrassment. "Well, let me take you out again, then? To make up for it?"

A small smile grew on her lips, but she forced it back down, as if it had snuck up on her. "I don't know. This is all a little too much."

"The Mallory thing? I didn't know she was your room-mate. I had no idea, I swear."

She scoffed. "She's my tenant. I own the place, rent out the two top floor bedrooms, and she's batshit crazy, so yeah, I'm a little concerned about the whole *you've-slept-with-my-roommate-who-will-probably-start-adding-Nair-to-my-shampoo* thing. Plus, you've got your family, and there are things going on there you can't or won't discuss. It's... a lot. And I'm just coming off a breakup myself. I need calm for a while and this isn't it."

173

"I know," I said. "I'm sorry. For the record, I wish it wasn't this way…" I was hit with a sudden pang of sadness for her and for what could've been if we'd met under different circumstances.

"Look, I know you're technically my boss and you could fire me for saying this, but…if you want your life to be something different than it is, just… God, fix it, Peter. It's your life, and absolutely no one has more control over it than you."

"Well, it's not that simple, is it? Some circumstances are out of my control."

"Then get them under your control," she said. "Don't hook up with random girls you don't know. Figure out your shit with your wife—stay in your marriage or get out, but quit straddling the line. People like to pretend they have no control over the way their life turns out, but the truth is that they just refuse to deal with the hard stuff because it's too painful and messy. You know what's even more painful and sticky? Prolonging bad situations for your own comfort. No one can solve your problems for you, Peter. No one wants to." She sighed, her eyes filling with sorrow. "Just…figure it out."

"I will," I promised her. "I am." At that moment, I knew she was right. No one had ever said it to me like that, but she was right. I needed the tough love she'd given me. I needed to take control. I needed to handle this. No longer was I going to let Ainsley control everything. I was an adult whose future was being decided by our next moves. I had every right to make decisions about our lives.

"Good," she said, then reached for the door. "You should go. I'll see you at work."

"Thank you," I said, shuffling across the room and out the door. I felt the urge to apologize again, but I resisted.

I walked out of the townhome, surprised to see Mallory waiting by my car. "Are you leaving?" she asked.

"Yeah, I should get going," I said hesitantly. "I shouldn't have come by. Listen, I'm sorry for..."

"Wasting my time? Making me look like an idiot? Embarrassing me in front of my roommate?"

"Yeah, that... I never meant to waste your time, Mallory. I had a lot of fun with you—"

"Don't," she cut me off. "I know who I am, okay? I know why men like you choose to match with me. I was nothing more than a one-nighter to you, and that's fine. But then you showed up here today all *Love, Actually*, and I thought 'hm, Mallory, maybe you were wrong about this one... Maybe he's one of the good guys.' I thought you were going to do some big romantic gesture like the fucking idiot I am."

"You're not—"

"But I was wrong, like always. You aren't one of the good guys, Pete. You aren't one of the good guys at all." She launched her foot back and kicked my car's bumper, cracking the plastic.

"What the hell?" I demanded, staring at her in disbelief.

"Serves you right," she huffed, storming past me. "Don't fucking contact me or come here ever again."

She slammed the door, and I stared at the crack in my bumper. *What the hell just happened?* I realized then that Gina likely hadn't been joking about Mallory adding Nair to her shampoo. I shook my head, forcing the thought away. A cracked bumper was the least of my worries, but I would fix that, too.

From here on out, I was going to fix things. I wasn't leaving it all up to Ainsley anymore. I was going to do things my way for a while. Whether she liked it or not.

CHAPTER TWENTY-SEVEN

AINSLEY

As I'd expected they would, the police pulled into our driveway that evening while Peter was out. I'd hoped Illiana would've kept her mouth shut, but I knew that wasn't likely to be the case.

The officer that stepped from the vehicle was around six foot tall, and wide, but made purely of muscle. His strong jaw and tough expression could be seen from where I stood at the door. His partner was short and thin, with red hair and freckles spattering his pale skin. It was hard not to notice the juxtaposition of the pair.

I opened the door before they reached me. "Hello. Can I help you, Officers?"

"Are you Ainsley Greenburg?" the short one asked.

"I am."

"I'm Officer Chad, and this is Officer Andrews," he said, gesturing toward his large and in charge, but oddly silent, partner. "We'd like to speak with you about Stefan De Luca."

"Of course, come inside." I held the door open wider, letting them past me. "Can I get you anything to drink?"

"That won't be necessary," Officer Andrews said, startling me with his booming voice. It matched his frame perfectly. "Let's take a seat."

I gestured toward the couch, and they sank down before I took my place across from them. "Illiana said they found his truck. Does that mean they found him? Is he okay?"

They exchanged a glance, and Officer Chad answered, "No, ma'am. We were able to locate his truck and they've begun to do DNA analysis, but there are no signs of Officer De Luca yet. Can you tell us what your relationship to Officer De Luca is?"

"Officer," I whispered the word, staring into space as it hit me, "that's right. He's a police officer, isn't he? I keep forgetting. Do you guys know him?"

Again, they exchanged a look, and Officer Andrews said, "We do, ma'am. We've worked with him for quite a while."

"And your relationship with him is…" Officer Chad went on, clicking his pen.

"Sorry, I, um, I don't really know him. We met on an app, Dater, and we went on a date last Tuesday. We'd messaged each other a few times, and I'm sure Illiana told you he came over on Friday night. But I never let him inside my house. We didn't talk, and he left a short while later. I haven't heard from him since."

"Why didn't you let him inside?"

"I, er," I rubbed a finger across my forehead, "I don't want to speak ill of your friend."

"Anything you can tell us at this point would be helpful to our investigation. We all want the same thing here."

"Well, to be honest, his messages had gotten a little... obsessive. I'm having problems with my marriage and I made a mistake, but I didn't want a relationship with him. It was just...like I said, it was a mistake. But Stefan didn't seem to understand that. At first I thought he was being nice, but then after he didn't stop messaging me when I was ignoring him, I started worrying about what he might do. I had no idea he was a cop, so when he learned my real name, I panicked. And then he showed up at my house... I didn't know what to do. I didn't feel safe letting him in. I wanted him to leave me alone."

"Did you tell him that?"

"I ignored him. I felt awful for leading him on."

"Is there anyone who can corroborate your story about that night?" Andrews asked.

"Besides Stefan?" I asked, furrowing my brows. "I don't think so. I called my husband to come home—he'd been working late—but by the time he got here, Stefan had gone. I hadn't heard from him since, so I assumed he'd given up. Then I saw the news."

"Is it possible your husband went after him after he left? Maybe he was angry that Officer De Luca had scared you?"

"No, no. Definitely not. Peter didn't leave my side that night after I called him to come home. I was too freaked out. And he had no idea what Stefan looked like or what he drove. He wouldn't have known how to find him or have had any reason to want to."

"I'm assuming he was angry about your affair, though?"

"No, he wasn't. We'd agreed to take some space, see other people, clear our heads. He wasn't mad about Stefan."

Officer Andrews scribbled something down while Officer Chad pressed on. "Is your husband here, by any chance? We'd love to get his take on a few things."

"He's not at the moment. He stepped out for a bit. Would you like me to call him and have him come home? It shouldn't take long for him to get here."

"Well, we'll get to that, but first, do you still have the messages between you and Officer De Luca? To give us some proof that what you're saying is true."

"Sure," I said, reaching over to the side table and pulling out my phone. I opened the Dater app and searched for his profile. As soon as I did, my heart sank. He was gone. His profile had disappeared.

My throat grew dry.

Then, with a wave of relief, I remembered that I had blocked him. I went to my settings and found him, hoping and praying that unblocking him would bring our old messages back up.

To my relief, it did. Once I could see the messages again, I held the phone out to the officers. "It starts here," I said, pointing to the conversation. "You can see where we first started talking, when he suggested we go out to eat, a message before we got there to say he was excited. Then, that night, he sent me a message to say he'd had a nice time and hoped to see me again. I didn't respond. Then, if you scroll down, you'll see the other messages he sent me.

He said he was thinking about me, said he'd hoped to go out again soon. Asked if he could call me. Then, when I still wasn't answering, the messages started coming more and more." I scrolled down, through the intense, incessant messages until we reached the end. The last message I had from him.

I'm outside. I need to see you.

The officers read through the messages, scrolling back up and reading them again. Officer Chad handed the phone back to me, clearing his throat. He appeared shaken. "And there are no other messages?"

"No. I didn't give him my phone number. Although, now that I think about it, I did have a few missed calls from a blocked number during the time he was messaging me, and I haven't had any since. Do you think those could've been him?"

"It's possible," he said. "We've been combing through his phone records, so we can find out."

I nodded. "I don't understand what he wanted from me. The date was mediocre at best."

The officers looked grim but didn't respond right away.

"Mrs. Greenburg, why didn't you contact us when you'd heard the news? You obviously knew that this information could've helped our investigation," Officer Chad said.

My heart fluttered. "To be honest, I was worried about it all coming out. Our marital issues. Seeing other people. It's embarrassing. I didn't want my kids to find out...or our coworkers, our friends. And, like I said, I truly don't have very much information at all." I hung my head.

"That's no excuse, I know. It was wrong. I should've come forward. Under any other circumstances, I would have. But I've told you everything I know now."

When I looked back up, they were watching me carefully, waiting to see if I'd say more. I cleared my throat.

"Do you still want me to call my husband?"

The wrinkle on Officer Andrews' forehead deepened as he leaned forward over his knees. "I don't think it'll be necessary, but if either of you do remember something else from that night, or from any of your other communications with Stefan De Luca, could you let us know?"

"Of course," I said. Officer Andrews held out a business card, and I tucked it into my pocket. "Thank you."

The men stood, making their way toward the door. "Thank you, ma'am. We'll get going now and out of your hair."

"I hope you find him," I offered sadly. "I hope he's okay."

They didn't turn around or respond as they continued out the door, and once they were pulling away, I waved casually. A few moments later, I saw Peter driving down the driveway, incredibly thankful he'd stayed gone long enough for me to get through the interview.

He'd surely have blown it.

I stepped outside and stuck my hands in my pockets, running the card between my fingers. *If I needed them, I could call.* I laughed to myself, tapping my foot on the wood of the porch. I could handle things just fine on my own.

CHAPTER TWENTY-EIGHT

PETER

When I got home, I was exhausted. My body was sore, my mind fuzzy and angry. I needed to sleep. I needed to shower off the crazy of the day. I walked through the garage, into the house, and up the stairs. Ainsley was standing in the hall with a strange expression on her face.

She didn't speak, didn't ask what I'd been up to. Perhaps she suspected she knew. Either way, I had no desire to recount the events of the night for her.

I walked into the bathroom and stripped out of my clothes, turning on the shower. After a few minutes, I heard the door open again and saw her walk inside through the beveled glass of the shower door.

"What's wrong?" I asked over the noise of the shower.

"The police were here," she said, her voice calm and cool.

I shut the water off, my body cold with shock. "What?"

"It's fine. I handled it."

She lifted her shirt over her head then stepped out of

her pants, pulling the door open and joining me in the long shower stall. She turned the water back on, turning the temperature up so the steam billowed around us.

For a long time, we just stood there, staring at each other. There was a kind of understanding there. We were in this together, and I think maybe we were both realizing that and fully accepting it. After a moment, she reached her hands out, wrapping them around my body.

The softness of her middle met the softness of mine, and we stood there, breathing and existing. I refused to think of anything else except how much I loved her. About what I would do to protect her.

When she pulled away, she trailed her hand down my stomach, her eyes meeting mine with unexpected, red-hot desire. I felt myself growing hard in reaction to the look in her eyes, even harder as her nails ran down my thigh.

I closed my eyes as she reached up, her hands gripping my neck as she kissed my lips softly. The kiss was gentle and sweet at first, then fiery all at once. A flame of passion exploded in my core, and I pulled away from her, spinning her around and shoving her into the wall. I pressed myself up against her back, my mouth on her neck, her shoulders. I bit down gently, then harder, applying pressure until she squealed. When she did, I let up, putting my mouth next to her ear as I entered her. I squeezed her breast, closing my eyes as I focused on her rhythmic breathing.

It was fast and hot, animalistic. There was no love in our sex right then, only pure passion, anger, and desire. I needed her, and she needed me. We let ourselves be used by the other.

When it was over, we collapsed together, sinking down to the floor of the shower, our bodies melded together as the water sprayed down on our stomachs. We lay there in silence for what seemed like an eternity before she turned her head to look at me, the water splashing in her face, droplets dripping off her nose and lips. Despite that, she barely blinked, almost oblivious to it happening.

She is so beautiful.

"You okay?" I asked, and she nodded.

"I just needed to remember."

"Remember?"

"Who we used to be…" she said.

I squeezed her arm, noticing the bright red bite mark on her otherwise perfect skin. "We're still those people."

"Are we? Or have we always been *these* people? Maybe we were only fooling ourselves in the beginning. Maybe this is the real version of us. This here."

I looked away from her, staring up at the ceiling with a heavy sigh. "Who can say what's real anymore, Ains? Real is what we make it." I gripped her shoulder. "This is real. The way I feel about you, that's real. Our kids are real. Whatever reality we want for ourselves, it can be real. We just have to fight like hell for it."

"Would you fight for me?" she asked, running a finger across my chest.

I turned my head, our eyes locking. "I'd kill for you, Ainsley. Without a second's hesitation."

She blinked, processing my words, and a small, sad smile filled her lips. "You already have."

I looked back at the ceiling, closing my eyes as the

water splashed on us. We could've fallen asleep, I was sure. Maybe we would. I could've lain there forever. As I felt sleep begin to pull me down into its dark, familiar abyss, I thought of Glennon's words, and they brought me back.

I'd kill for you, but I can't tell you the truth.

I knew I had to tell her the truth, though. As much as it was going to kill me. She needed to hear it from me. Glennon's countdown had begun, and I wasn't planning on waiting out the clock.

I had to tell her soon.

CHAPTER TWENTY-NINE

AINSLEY

The next afternoon, as I waited in the elementary school pick-up line on a rare occasion when the kids didn't have any after-school plans, my phone rang. A glance at the screen told me it was Glennon.

"Hello?"

"Hey, babe. How are you?"

"I'm okay," I said through a yawn. "Just picking up the kids from school." I slowed to a stop in the pick-up lane and leaned back to grin at Maisy as she opened the car door. I mouthed, "Hello," and pointed to the screen. She smiled and waved at me as she climbed into the vehicle and joined her brothers in the backseat. "Auntie Glennon's on the phone, say hi!"

"Hi," came the echoed response.

When they shut the door, I turned back to Glennon. "Sorry, is everything okay?"

"Oh, yeah, definitely. I wanted to check in. I can call back later."

"No need to, what's up?"

"I, um, well, it's fine. I'll call you back."

"Ah," I said, turning off the Bluetooth from the car and moving the phone to my ear. "Okay, you're off Bluetooth now. It's just us. What's *really* up?"

"It's nothing important. I didn't want to worry the kids. I was calling to see if things are getting better between you two?"

"Peter and me?"

"Yeah," she said with a dry laugh. "Who else?"

"Oh, yeah, I guess so. I don't know. Things feel so strange right now. I mean, it's fine, of course. It's just... We're in a weird place." I met Maisy's eye in the mirror, and despite my attempt to code what I was saying, she seemed to have figured me out. I changed the subject. "It was so nice to get to see you guys, though. We enjoyed ourselves."

Glennon was silent.

"You there?"

"Yeah, I just, uh, it may be the last time you see us, together..."

"What do you mean?" I asked. "Why would it be the last time?"

She sighed, and I heard the tears in her voice when she responded. "I'm leaving Seth."

"You're *what?* Wait, why? What's going on? You guys seemed so great."

"Yeah," she sniffled, "well, looks can be deceiving."

"What's going on, Glen? Tell me."

"I don't want to bother you when you're with the kids. I figured they were out with friends or something, and I wanted to catch you before you got home. I'm sorry, I'm just...I'm a mess."

"Where are you? Are you at home?"

"Yeah, I am. I'm getting ready to go stay at my mom's for a few weeks—maybe a few months—until we get things sorted out."

I gripped the steering wheel. "Wait, so this is, this is real? I mean, you're moving out? Now?"

"Yeah. I've been debating for a few weeks, but I can't pretend anymore. I'm moving in with Mom, and he'll stay at the house until we can sell it. Neither of us can afford to buy the other out, so it's the only way. With no kids and the house being our only asset, I think it'll be pretty simple. I don't want any part of his company or income. I just want out."

"But I don't... I don't understand. What happened? Why didn't you tell me any of this?"

"I've been waiting for you to have less going on. I didn't want to be a burden, but I wanted to tell you before it's official." She was crying again. "You're like my sister, Ains. I love you so much, and I never want to hurt you or lie to you. I want you to know what's going on..."

"I'm not mad at you, Glennon. You don't have to worry about that. You never have to tell me anything until you're ready. I'm having trouble understanding. Did something happen or... I mean, did you grow apart? Where is this all coming from?"

She was crying again, sobbing actually. "I'm...sorry..."

"Shhh," I tried to soothe her. "Listen, I'm coming to you, okay? I'm going to drop the kids off at home with

Peter and head your way. I'm about fifteen minutes away from the house—"

"No, no! You don't need to do that."

"I want to," I said.

"You should spend time with the kids."

"You need me—hey, Glennon, can I call you right back?" I asked as I was interrupted by an incoming call from Peter. "Peter's calling me."

"Yeah, sure."

"Okay, I'll talk to you in a bit." With that, I ended the call and switched to the one that was incoming. "Hello?"

"Hey."

"Peter?" I asked. "What's wrong? Is everything okay?"

"Where are you?"

"I'm almost home. Did something happen?"

His tone was dry. "Uh, yeah, you could say that. You haven't heard the news?"

I felt a knot growing in my stomach, my heart beginning to race. I knew by the tone of his voice, whatever it was couldn't be good. I gripped the steering wheel tighter, bracing myself.

"What news?"

"It's all over the place."

"What is? What's going on?" I asked, pressing my lips into a thin line as I forced myself to breathe.

"It's Illiana De Luca," he said, pausing. "She's—Ainsley, she's missing."

CHAPTER THIRTY

PETER

W hen Ainsley made it home, she rushed inside, hanging her jacket and bag on the coat rack in the hall, and hurried toward me. I smiled at the kids, trying not to let them know anything was wrong, though they didn't seem to care either way. Only Riley asked whether I'd had a good day, but as soon as I'd said yes and asked about his, the kids had all disappeared to their rooms, and I was able to return to my pacing of the hallway.

The television in the living room was on, though the station was on a commercial.

"Okay," Ainsley said, reaching for my arms to stop me from moving. She put a hand on either of my biceps, squaring her body to mine. I felt my heartbeat slowing. "Talk to me. What happened?"

I led her into the living room, gesturing toward the TV.

"They can't find her," I said. "The police said she's wanted for questioning regarding her husband's disappearance, and they can't find her. Her phone and wallet were found at home. Her SUV was there. She's just...she's gone."

"Okay," she said, letting the news wash over her. "But, isn't that a good thing? I mean, I hope she's okay, but if she's wanted for questioning, that means they don't suspect anyone else, right?"

"Maybe," I said, "but even so, if she was a suspect and now she's gone, they'll be coming back to us."

"But we didn't have anything to do with this. Really this time."

I nodded. "I know that, but how are we going to prove it?"

"We don't have to prove anything right now. For all we know, the police have moved on. When they left last night, I'd proved that Stefan was all but stalking me and that we had nothing to do with his disappearance. Maybe they have moved on to Illiana as a suspect and, if she's even missing, we need to wait it out and see what they have to say. There's no need to panic."

I nodded, feeling like there was definitely *some* need to panic, but I didn't say as much. Instead, I pressed my lips to her forehead. "I'm sorry I'm stressing. I just..."

"I know," she said. "I'm worried, too, but we have to try to keep it together. Both of us. Falling apart right now doesn't solve anything."

"I know you're right." I gathered my hands at my chest, rubbing circles with my thumb on the opposite palm. "I'm freaking out," I said wildly, unable to hold the panic in any longer.

"Where were you last night?" she asked, shocking me

back to reality. It was the first time she'd brought it up, and I didn't like the way she was asking.

"Out. I went out."

"Out where? Come on, I need to know in case the police do come around."

I sighed. "I went to grab a beer."

"Okay, good. Where did you go? Somewhere where there'll be camera footage?"

"Er, well, I didn't end up getting in anywhere. That was where I was headed, but I drove around instead. I needed to clear my head."

She nodded but kept her eyes trained on mine. "If there's one thing we don't need right now, it's to lie to each other. We're on the same side. Like we said yesterday. We'd do anything for each other. It's us versus them, always."

"I'm not lying," I swore. "I drove around. That was it."

She studied me, an unreadable expression on her face. "So you didn't do this?"

"Didn't do what? Th-the Illiana thing? You think I... what? You think I did something to her? Are you seriously asking me that?"

"You were gone a long time, Peter. And you were the one saying we needed to take care of the problem."

"I didn't mean that we should *kill her*. You can't be serious right now, Ainsley. Who do you think I am?" I put a hand over my forehead. "I would never... I mean, what I did to... I feel sick about it. I hate myself. I would never do it again." I put my hand over my stomach, feeling ill as I thought about it. "I physically couldn't."

"Okay," she said, the end of her word an octave higher than the rest, as if she were asking a question.

"What? You don't believe me?"

"I don't know what to believe, Peter. I *want* to believe you."

"Well, what about you? Where were you?"

"I was home," she said angrily. "And don't you dare point fingers at me. You'd have known where I was if you hadn't stormed out."

"I needed air, Ainsley. Is that a crime?"

"No," she said, "but murder is."

I swallowed, hearing the hint of threat in her voice. "I don't want to fight. That's not what we should be doing right now," I croaked out. "I love you. Us against them, right?"

She didn't answer or fight against it as I pulled her in for a hug, but she didn't return the hug either. "I should go anyway."

"*Go?* Go where?" I stepped back.

"I'm supposed to go check on Glennon. She needs me."

I swallowed, feeling the fear swoop in again. "Why does she need you?"

She bounced her head back and forth, contemplating. "If I tell you, you can't tell Seth you know. Not yet."

"Know what?" I could barely utter the words.

"She's leaving him."

The statement hit me like a ton of bricks. "Excuse me?"

"Glennon's leaving Seth. She's moving into her mom's house."

"W-why? What happened? How long have you known?"

"I found out like a second before I got home, and I have no idea what happened. I got off the phone to answer your call, but I told her I'd be over as soon as I could. She's in a rough place. I'm not sure when I'll be back. Probably late." She was making her way back toward the door. *We had a week. She promised me a week.* "Are you okay with the kids for the evening?"

"Wait, Ainsley. *Wait.*" I reached for her arm, grabbing it harder than I'd meant to. She spun around, glaring at me.

"What? I need to go. She's waiting." She jerked her arm out of my grip.

"There's something we need to talk about. S-something I need to tell you."

"Okay," she said, cocking her hip to the side as she waited.

"It's—can you sit down?"

"You're scaring me…" She eased herself toward the couch and sank down. "What is it?"

"I…" I sat down next to her, putting my head in my hands. *"Fuck."* It hurt to even let myself think the words, let alone say them aloud. "I'm an idiot. I'm a fucking idiot."

"What are you talking about?" she asked, and I felt her hand graze my shoulder. I shoved it off, shaking my head as hot tears filled my eyes. I didn't deserve her comfort.

"You're going to hate me."

"I could never hate you…" she whispered. "I love you, Peter. Nothing you could ever say would change that."

"I hope you mean that, but I don't think you do."

"Spit it ou—"

"I've been cheating on you," I said, a grimace on my face as I lifted my head from my hands. "With Seth."

CHAPTER THIRTY-ONE

AINSLEY

I stared at my husband as he said the seven words I'd never, not in a million years, expected him to say. The words washed over me, coursing in and out of my ear like a heartbeat. I heard them over and over.

I've been cheating on you.

With Seth.

I've been cheating on you.

With Seth.

I've been cheating on you.

With Seth.

I couldn't speak. I stood up, walking away from him with one hand on my stomach, the other on my chest. I felt as though I'd been kicked square in my core.

"Ainsley, I—"

I whipped around to stare at him, cutting his sentence short. "*Seth* Seth? Glennon's husband? My best friend's husband? Are you serious? You can't be serious... Is this a joke?"

He winced as I doled out the questions, hanging his head. "I'm so sorry."

"Does Glennon know?"

"She just found out."

"So that's why…" I trailed off, looking around the room. It was as if the world I'd woken up in no longer existed. As if I'd been picked up and dropped into a new world where nothing I thought I knew was true. "How could you do this to me? I mean, are you like… Are you coming out to me right now? What is this, Peter? How could I not know you are gay? *Are you gay?*" Nothing made sense. *"Seth?"* I couldn't catch my breath.

"I'm not gay," he said, almost defensively. "I'm…well, I guess I'm bisexual. Seth's the only man I've ever been with. I've always been…interested, I guess, but Seth…I don't know. It was different with him. *He* was different."

"How can this be happening?" I sank down onto my knees on the floor, the questions flowing out of me. "Are you leaving me? Are you asking me for a divorce? Do you want to be with him? Does he want to be with you? Are you leaving us for each other?"

"No," he said, sinking down directly in front of me. He reached for my hands where they rested on my knees, but I jerked them away. "No. Ainsley, look at me." He placed his hands on either side of my cheeks, gently urging me to meet his eye. "I'm not leaving you. I love you. I love our family. I love our kids. With Seth, it was just…" He took a deep breath. "It's not an affair. It was a mistake. A stupid, stupid mistake."

"When did it happen?"

"A few months ago, the first time. And twice since

then." He put his face in his hands. "I felt awful. I've wanted to tell you... It's been eating me up. And then when you suggested we see other people, I guess I thought maybe you'd be okay with it. And then Glennon found out and made me promise to tell you... I'm so sorry, Ainsley."

"So you weren't going to tell me if Glennon hadn't made you?"

"I would've!" he insisted, but he was clearly lying. "Just not in the middle of all of this." His face crinkled as he cried, silent tears streaming out of his eyes. As much as I felt anger and resentment toward him, I had to give him the freedom to tell me the truth.

"Are you sure you don't want to be with him? Are you sure you don't love him? I could never hate you for choosing to be honest with yourself. I'm hurt, don't get me wrong, but I don't want you to hide who you are if—"

"It's not," he cut me off, grabbing my hands. "It's not who I am. Who I am is your husband. The man who loves you more than life itself."

"Is Seth leaving Glennon for you?"

"I have no idea," he said, putting his head down again. "I don't think so. I've told him we can't be serious. I've told him I love you."

I tilted my head to the side, trying to process all I was being told. "She must be so devastated..."

"She is, but not for the reasons you think," he said, drawing my attention back to him.

"What does that mean?"

"She's worried about you—"

"I'm fine! She needs to worry about her own marriage..."

"Why do you think Glennon's always got her nose in our business, Ainsley? In our marriage? Why do you think she's always trying to fix our problems and make sure we're perfect?"

"Because she's my best friend."

He gave me a patronizing look, leaning forward so our faces were merely inches apart. "Because she doesn't have her own marriage to worry about."

"What are you talking about?"

"Seth's gay, Ainsley. A hundred percent gay. Never slept with a woman in his life."

"That's impossible—"

"It's not. Ask Glennon. Ask her, and she'll tell you the truth."

"But...I don't understand. Why would she marry him if that's the case? Why would she be leaving him now? Did she know when they got married? She had to if..."

"She's always known. It's why they don't have kids, why he's always away on business trips. Seth's family are devout Catholics. When he came out, they threatened to take him out of the will, take away his trust fund, if he didn't marry a woman."

"That's...awful," I said, feeling my anger dissipating. "Poor Seth... But I don't understand. If that's the case, why didn't Glennon tell me? Why would she agree to it in the first place?"

"I guess they're just good friends," he said. "You know Glennon cares about other people way too much. She's always the first to jump up and sacrifice herself for the greater good. She's always taking care of you, and the kids... Seth needed help, she was his best friend, and she helped him. From what Seth says, it was as simple as that. Plus, Glennon's been taken care of. He's not the only one benefiting from their arrangement. Seth was able to get her the best care when she was sick all that time. And he's been funding her nonprofit since it opened. It was a trade-off, and they've been making it work all these years."

I nodded. What he was saying made sense in a weird way, but I still felt like I was in an alternate reality. It all felt like it was some big joke. Like Glennon and Seth were going to jump out of the kitchen any minute, laughing about how hard I'd fallen for it.

How had I missed it? I'd seen them together so many times. How had I not picked up on the fact that they weren't...*together* in that way? I'd seen them kiss, hadn't I? I thought back, recalling several pecks on the cheek and forehead. Nothing more. Then again, who makes out in front of their friends? It wasn't the weirdest thing to be a bit private.

But Glennon wasn't private about anything else...

"So, if she knew he was gay, I guess I don't understand. Why is she leaving him now?"

"Because of you, Ainsley. Because he hurt you. Because *I* hurt you. If there's one thing she could never forgive, it's anyone hurting you."

I thought back to what she'd said on the phone, remembering her tears coming as she'd said she didn't want to lie to me or hurt me. Realization swept through me as every piece of the puzzle clicked into place. It was my turn to put my face in my hands, trying to pull myself together.

"Oh my God..." I whispered breathlessly. No other phrase seemed to fit the way I was feeling.

"She said you told her you'd leave me if I cheated on you," Peter whispered, touching my arm.

"That is what I said," I told him, nodding in my hands.

"Is that still the truth? Do you want to leave me?"

"I just...need time, Peter. You can't ask me that right now."

"Please, Ainsley. Please don't do this. I love you." I looked up, watching a tear drip off the end of his nose. "Please. This is it. This is our moment of total honesty. We get all our secrets out, and then we move on. We can do it. I know we can. We have to. I can't lose you."

I moved to stand up. "I can't, Peter. I can't do this right now. I need to go see Glennon. I need to be with her. I need to make sense of this all."

He reached for my hand. "Wait." His grip tightened.

"Let me go!" I cried, jerking it away from him at the exact moment I heard a knock on the door.

Both our eyes widened as we looked toward the sound. Peter walked past me, wiping his eyes and putting a hand up to keep me back as he pulled open the door. "Can I help you?" he asked.

I walked around him until I could see who was standing there, surprised to see the officers had come back. Maybe Peter had been right after all... With Illiana gone, would they start looking at us again? Maybe they'd never stopped.

"Are you Peter Green—" As Officer Chad recognized

me, he stopped short. "Good evening, Mrs. Greenburg. Did we catch you at a bad time?"

I sniffled and ran a finger under my eyes. "No, of course not. Officers, this is my husband, Peter," I said, a lump of fear forming in my chest. "Please, come in."

They stepped over the threshold, but this time, they didn't sit down when I gestured that they should. Instead, Officer Chad nodded at Peter, then at me, and began to speak. "I'm sorry to bother you all. We won't be staying long. We came by because I'm afraid we have some unfortunate news…"

I squared my shoulders, bracing myself for whatever was coming.

"As you may have heard, Illiana De Luca has gone missing."

"We did hear, yeah," I confirmed when he paused. "It was on the news."

"Good. Okay, well, what I'm about to tell you hasn't been released to the public yet, but we wanted to give you a heads-up before it is." He sighed, looking around the room. "Are your children home?"

"They are, but they're in their rooms. Do I need to get them?" My heart fluttered at the thought. I didn't want to involve them. Were they going to arrest us? Would the kids need to go to CPS? I wrung my hands together in front of my waist.

"No, it's better that they're not here. They don't need to hear what I'm about to tell you. It's not…it's not the kind of news we like to give."

"I'm afraid I don't understand," I said. Beside me, Peter was being quiet, for which I was grateful. I had built a rapport with the officers, I could tell. They trusted me somewhat. They held eye contact with me whenever they spoke.

"Ma'am, there's no easy way to say this. We have reason to believe Stefan De Luca is a serial rapist."

I took a sharp breath, stepping backward, my knees nearly giving out under me. "He wh—"

"Inside his truck, we found a bag filled with several pairs of women's underwear. We're making an attempt to identify them, but we also found a rope that matches the ligature marks we've found on numerous victims over the past several years. It has a distinctive pattern of small, metal rings around it... In every case, the victim's underwear had been removed. We've believed for quite some time that the perpetrator had been collecting them."

"Collecting..." I bent down, trying to steady myself as I processed what they were telling us.

"I realize this is hard to hear, ma'am. We're only telling you because we wanted to be sure Officer De Luca didn't do anything inappropriate during your time together. We know that he's a fellow officer, but please don't think that will mean we won't prosecute him to the full extent of the law when we find him, or that we won't take your accusations seriously. I know you said he was kind to you on your date, but if you'd been lying for any reason, now's the time to tell us. It could mean the difference in saving a life."

I shook my head.

"No, he...he didn't. He wasn't... Um, he...he was the perfect gentleman."

The officers exchanged a glance and nodded. Officer

Andrews said, "Then I'd say you were very lucky, ma'am." His tone was kind, but I couldn't bear to look at him.

I blinked rapidly, rubbing my eyes as my breathing grew irregular. I put a hand over my chest, squeezing my eyes shut as I tried to focus.

"And...and Illiana? Did he...did he hurt her?" I looked up at them.

If it were possible, Officer Chad's face grew more grim as he prepared to answer the question.

"*We believe...*" He seemed hesitant to say more, and I worried, briefly, that he wouldn't. "We believe Mrs. De Luca has been...involved in her husband's crimes. Whether or not she planned them or helped him carry them out, we aren't sure. When we asked Mrs. De Luca about the bag, she claimed not to know anything about it. But now, she's gone missing, too. We're very concerned that she may be on the run, but we can't be sure of anything right now."

"As we've said," Officer Andrews added, "it's an ongoing investigation, and this is all sensitive information, which is why we'd appreciate your discretion with what we're telling you. "

"Why *are* you telling us this, though? What have we got to do with any of it?" Peter asked, finding his voice.

It was Officer Andrews who answered. "Because we believe your wife was meant to be De Luca's next victim. Now, she may be perfectly safe, but we wanted to warn you that if either of them were to contact you, we'd like you to call us straight away. Don't talk to them, don't engage. Call us or, if you believe you're in immediate danger, say if they were to show up here again, call 911. Do you still have our number?"

I nodded. "Yes, of course."

"Good. We're going to have an officer patrol your area for the next few nights to be on the lookout, but you need to be vigilant as well. The De Lucas have done extensive research on you. They know where you work, where you live... From what we're discovering, they are very dangerous people. Do you understand what I'm saying?"

I nodded again, unable to speak.

"Do you have any questions for us? Anything else we should know?"

I shook my head as I felt Peter's arm slink around me. He rested his chin on the top of my head.

"Thank you, Officers."

The men nodded, making eye contact with him, then me.

"Take care now. And be safe." With that, they saw themselves out, leaving us in silence as what we'd been told sank in.

Peter spun me around after a moment, looking me in the eye.

"Did he try something with you?" I pulled myself from his grasp. "You need to tell me the truth."

"No, Peter, of course not. I would've told you."

"You swear it?"

"I swear," I told him.

"I'd never forgive myself if something happened to you."

"I was fine. He didn't try anything."

"I can't lose you, Ainsley. God, I don't know what I'd do if—"

"You won't," I promised. "We're in this together, right?"

"Together," he said, pulling me into his chest. "You and me."

I squeezed him tighter, feeling our hearts beating together. "But you can't lie to me anymore, Peter. No more secrets between us. I can't handle any more. Our marriage can't survive any more. We have to both agree."

"No more secrets," he said. "I promise you. No more secrets, no more lies. If we can survive what we've survived over these last few days, we can survive anything."

At his words, I pulled away, staring up at him.

"Are you sure?"

"I love you, Ainsley. I will fight for you every single day. I'm not letting you go. Not now, not ever."

"You swear it?" I asked, pinching the skin around my nails. "We can forgive each other for anything?"

"If you can forgive me for what I did, I will never let you go. I'm in this with you if you're in it with me." He kissed my lips. "We can be the people we were before. Is that what you want? Can you forgive me? Can we work through this together?"

I looked down, pinching my cuticle again. As I broke the skin, I looked down, staring as the blood began to pool. I watched the red dot as it grew, spilling out into the crevices of my thumb nail.

"Ainsley?" Peter said, and I got the impression he'd already said my name once. I'd been lost in my thoughts. "Can you forgive me?"

"I can," I said softly, chewing on my bottom lip as I swiped my bloody thumb onto my pants. "If you can forgive me."

The smile faded from his face. "Forgive you for what?"

"For what I'm about to tell you…" I whispered, my chin quivering. I wasn't sure I'd be able to form the words.

"What is it? What do you have to tell me?"

"You should sit," I said. "It's about Stefan. About why he died. About why I had to do it."

"Why you had to do what?"

I pressed my lips together, inhaling deeply through my nose. "I had no idea what I was doing. I didn't think it would actually work. I didn't know if I could pull it off. I mean, it's a relief, right? Knowing that we're going to get away with it. Knowing that we actually pulled it off and they don't suspect us. I'd been living with such guilt and worry and—"

"What are you talking about, Ainsley? You aren't making sense… I mean, sure, it's a relief that they don't think I killed him, but I wouldn't say we're off the hook just—"

"That's just it, Peter. That's what I'm trying to tell you."

"What are you trying to tell me?" he asked, letting a desperate, breathy sigh escape his throat.

"You didn't kill Stefan." I took another deep breath, stilling my shaking hands. "I did," I said. And then, I told him everything.

CHAPTER THIRTY-TWO

PETER

I stared at my wife, listening to a story that came straight from a nightmare. It wasn't possible, and yet, she'd have no reason to lie. No reason to make herself look like such a monster. I wasn't sure how to feel about it.

Rage? Of course.

Relief that I knew the truth? I wasn't sure.

Relief that she was alive? Above all else.

"I had to do it. I had to fix us. I needed to come up with a solution... I know it sounds stupid, but I needed you to...to owe me."

"Owe you?" I furrowed my brow. "What the fuck does that even mean?"

"I knew about your affairs. All of them, or so I thought. I knew you were sleeping around. Not with Seth," she added, as I felt my heart plummet. "He was the one you managed to keep from me. But I knew about the others. I'd seen the photos on your phone. I'd followed you a few times when you'd left the house to meet them."

"I don't...I don't understand."

"I was so angry with you. So angry. I'd been good to you. I'd been faithful. I'd stood by your side while you built a company. I'd given you three beautiful children, a beautiful home, and... I still wasn't enough for you."

"You were enough for me, you *are*!" I told her, feeling my body begin to tremble. I didn't know whether to feel more angry or afraid. I'd sworn to her I had no more secrets, and she knew I'd been lying. So why did I need to forgive her? She should be the one forgiving me...

"I was heartbroken. I wanted to pay you back for the way I felt. I wanted you to *hurt*. I wanted you to have no choice but to stay with me. I told you when we got married, I'd never let you go. I never wanted to be a divorcée. I didn't want what our parents have."

"I don't want that either..."

"So, when I suggested we see other people, I did it deliberately. I wasn't sure if it was going to work, but I had a plan. One of the first questions I asked my matches was what they did for a living, because I knew what I needed. Stefan being a cop wasn't an accident. He was so proud of his work, and I knew he would take me seriously when I told him my story. On our date, I told him that I was married. I told him my real name, though I pretended that was an accident. I told him that..." She paused.

"That what?"

"I told him that you were controlling. That you'd...that you'd hit me a few times."

"You what?" I screamed, leaping from the couch as anger overtook me. "Jesus fucking Christ, Ainsley. Why

the hell would you do that? I've never laid a finger on you."

"I know," she said, wincing. "I know. It's just...I needed him to worry. I told him that I was trying to leave you, and that I needed to meet people and remember who I was before I married you. I told him that I was worried you'd do something awful, but that you had all the money and I was worried you'd take the kids if I didn't stay with you."

"Ainsley..." I shook my head, running my hands through my hair incessantly. How was any of this possible? What was she telling me? "He was a cop. He could've come and arrested me."

"I made him swear not to tell. I told him I could handle it. That I needed a friend. It was awful, I know. And, the worst part is, when I left, I purposely didn't message him back because I wanted him to come looking for me. I wanted him to worry about me. And when he came to the house, he just wanted to make sure I was okay. I didn't know that you'd go through with it. I mean, I hoped you would. I hoped you'd be so scared and you'd have the bat... I hoped you'd protect me, but I couldn't be sure... I know you so well, but I can't always predict your moves. But when you did, when you did exactly what I'd hoped for, I knew I had you. I knew that secret...that was the kind of secret we'd take to our graves. Together. Because we *are* in it together."

Her face grew stony, though her tone remained sad. "For better or worse. Because your only choice now is to kill me yourself or stay with me forever. I own your secret now, Peter. I own you."

I swallowed, standing from the couch and stepping back away from her. "So he was never going to hurt you?"

"That's just it. Didn't you hear what the cops said? If he was a rapist, then he actually *was* going to hurt me. You did save me, Peter. You saved my life. Right? If he was going to do something awful…"

I shook my head, my vision tunneling as I tried to make sense of it all. "You didn't have to do this. I was never going to leave you."

She stood, walking toward me. "No, but you were going to keep cheating on me and lying to me. Don't you see? It's fixed now. We're fixed now. All the secrets are out on the table."

She gave a wide grin, as if she was proud of what she'd done. "We can be the people we were again. We can fall in love with who we are now. This is a fresh start for us. You promised we could get through anything as long as we were honest with each other. You promised we could fight to get back to who we were. As long as there are no more lies, and there aren't. I've told you everything."

"I don't know if I can move past this, Ains…"

"You can," she said simply. "You have to. *We* have to. I've forgiven you, Peter. For Seth. For all the women. All the lies. You *can* forgive me for this. We can move past it. You said if I told you everything, you'd still love me. You said we'd be together forever. This is our moment of total honesty. We get all the secrets out, and then we move forward. That's what you said."

"Yeah, but I never expected anything like this… You made me kill someone, Ainsley. All for your sick mind games."

"I didn't make you do anything. You're the one who swung the bat."

"Because you told me that he was—"

"What's done is done," she said, swiping her hand through the air as if dusting our problem away. "I'm the one who knows where the murder weapon is. Where the body is. I'm the one who can tell the police what happened that night. And who do you think they'll believe? The jealous husband? Or the wife who went out with a serial rapist and lived to tell the tale?"

She reached out, running a finger down my chest, her nail digging into my skin through my shirt. "Nothing can ever come between us now, don't you see that? If we can love each other through all of the darkness, we'll be able to survive anything. I've given us a gift. I've made our sins equal. I do love you, Peter. I've never stopped. Once the anger fades, I know you'll see it too. I know you love me."

She pressed up onto her tiptoes and kissed my lips. I didn't resist, but I didn't kiss her back. When we broke apart, she appeared unbothered and tapped a finger to the end of my nose. "No more secrets. Just honesty and love."

She lowered herself, gave me a small smile, and walked away. I heard the shuffling of her feet across the hardwood in the kitchen. And then, like so many nights before, as if this night wasn't any different, she called, "I still need to go check on Glennon. Can you handle dinner?"

CHAPTER THIRTY-THREE

SIX MONTHS LATER

"Glennon's on the phone," I called to Peter, leaning my head out the door. "She and her mom are in Panama City. She wants to know if you want a blue or red shirt from the gift shop."

He lifted his head up from where he was working in the yard. "Tell her to surprise me."

"Can do," I said, closing the door. "Did you hear that?"

She giggled. "I did. One glittery pink shirt coming up."

"Has Seth gotten down there yet?"

"He's coming down tomorrow after he gets back from Salt Lake City."

"How do you think he's doing?" I asked. I'd been concerned about him, though not concerned enough to invite him around. Not yet. I wanted Glennon to find her footing, to guide us in the direction she wanted to go. Would we ever be friends like we were before? I didn't know. I could no longer trust him. But with time, I was learning, all things could be healed.

"I don't know," she said. "I think he's happier, but I know his parents are struggling with it. The business is doing well, though. They just bought out a little mom-and-pop shop in Vegas. So what if he lost his trust fund? He doesn't need it anymore. What he needs is to be happy. We both do. I'm glad we're back to something cordial, though... I've missed him. "

"I'm sure you have, and I know he's happy to be seeing you again," I said. "I'm glad to see you happy. Whatever that means."

"Thanks, friend. I love ya. I'm gonna get off of here and pay for this adorable pink shirt I'm surprising Peter with," she said with a boisterous laugh.

I smiled, shaking my head. "Okay, we'll see you in a week. Love ya." I ended the call and grabbed the two glasses of lemonade I'd prepared. The summer was coming in quickly, and it was rare to find a day under ninety degrees anymore.

We'd waited to start our latest project until the investigation surrounding Stefan and Illiana's disappearances had died down. Though neither of them had been located, the news was reporting that the police believed the two of them could have crossed the border either north or south. A few months ago, the police had stopped patrolling the area, giving us our freedom and peace of mind back.

And Peter and I were better. We were trying true counseling this time, and it seemed to be helping.

Total honesty.

No more secrets.

That was our new philosophy. No more lies, even when they hurt.

Our marriage had become...interesting to say the least, but we were in it for the long haul, and that was all I could ask for. Besides, the sex had become phenomenal, usually ending with a few bruises, bite marks, and occasionally some blood.

Neither of us seemed to mind.

What we'd gone through had awakened something in us both. We were wild now, free and open with each other in a way we'd never been before. We parented differently, embraced life as it came. I didn't worry about all that I'd never get back, choosing instead to look forward to all I still had coming.

I wanted to live my life. I wanted to explore. And I wanted to do it all with Peter by my side.

"Here you go," I told him, handing over both glasses of lemonade before I jumped down from the edge of the porch. I took mine back once I'd landed and sank down in the lawn chair, watching him as he drank his glass. He leaned over, propping his arm against the handle of the garden hoe he'd been using to smooth the new concrete patio in our front yard.

The kids had been all too happy to disappear for the day, especially when we'd asked them for help tearing up the front porch to make way for our new project.

That left the house to ourselves and a full day to get our new patio completed. We'd been working tirelessly, but as the afternoon sun had begun to set, the concrete had been laid and smoothed. All that was left, after the concrete dried, was to build a small set of stairs from the little section of our porch that remained down onto the concrete slab.

It had been the biggest wave of relief—the moment Peter began pouring the concrete, the moment I realized we were actually going to get away with this. It was as if a weight had been lifted off my shoulders.

Suddenly, nothing mattered.

We'd gotten through it.

We'd survived.

Peter walked over to me, bending down and kissing me square on the mouth. I leaned forward, pressing my lips to his. The kiss lingered, causing me to lose myself in the moment. When we broke apart, he smiled at me lovingly and ran a hand through my hair, then plopped down on the grass next to me, wiping the sweat from his brow.

"Well, what do you think, Mrs. Greenburg?"

"It looks amazing," I told him. "Seriously, you'd think you were an architect or something."

He laughed. "Well, it's not half as good as my team could've done, but you should see the blueprint."

"We'll have to hang it up," I teased.

"I'm glad to have it done," he said. "I feel like I can breathe again."

I sipped my lemonade, staring out at the sun as it set. "Same."

He reached for my hand, squeezing it gently. "Thank you," he said, catching me off guard.

"For what?" I asked with a soft laugh.

"For fixing me. For fixing us. I may not agree with your methods, but they worked. You fixed our marriage,

Ainsley. You fixed me. Made me better. If not for you, I'd still be out there…lost. Messing things up for us."

"I fix things, honey. And you happen to be my favorite thing to fix." I winked at him, pursing my lips. He set his glass down, smiling up at me and jerking his head in the opposite direction, begging me to come sit next to him.

When I stood, he pulled me down onto his lap, kissing me deeply, his breath heavy. His sweat rubbed off on me as my lemonade spilled, but neither of us cared. We rolled in the grass, kissing and exploring like two teenagers.

He was right, I'd fixed us.

And I had zero regrets.

CHAPTER THIRTY-FOUR

PETER

A fter the sun had set, Ainsley went inside to clean up before dinner. The concrete was dry, though not fully set. In the morning, I'd build the stairs, and it would be done. Before I joined her inside, I walked into the garage, putting the tools away.

I couldn't stop smiling as I put them back in their places. I never thought I'd see the day when my wife would let me have my way with her on the front lawn, but I was a lucky man. I couldn't believe I'd almost thrown that all away.

I meant what I'd said. Every word. Ainsley had saved me. She'd told me her whole truth—bared her soul to me. Her deepest darkest secrets. We knew everything about each other.

Well, almost everything. But there were some things she could never know. Some things that were unforgivable. Too terrible to say out loud.

I laid the half-empty bag of unused concrete in the corner, checked behind me to be sure the coast was clear, and bent down. I shoved the shelf down a half inch, running my fingers along the brick wall until I found the right one.

I pushed in on the first loose brick, then stood and pressed one three squares up. I followed the pattern carefully and, when I pressed the last brick, the wall popped open just a hair. I stuck my fingers in the gap, opening the hidden door, and stepping inside the dark room. I pulled it closed behind me before flipping on the light.

The room was practically a lair, something I'd meticulously designed when I'd created the blueprint for the house. Totally sound and weatherproofed, and thin enough that it fit easily along the side of the house without anyone—Ainsley included—ever suspecting it was there.

I walked across the damp concrete, drying from the vigorous clean it'd had the night before. I made my way toward the freezer, noticing a smear of blood on the edge of the lid that I'd missed.

I grabbed the spray bottle of bleach from the metal table next to the freezer and sprayed it down, using a paper towel to clean it thoroughly. Not that anyone would ever see it, but I liked to have a clean space. It was important to me. I opened the freezer, pulling out the pearl bracelet that sat at the bottom, waiting for me.

I ran the pearls between my fingers as I walked to the far corner of the room. It was dimly lit, practically unnoticeable, but it held my most prized possession. I pulled out the built-in drawer from the wall, sized perfectly to fit the black duffel bag I'd gotten seventeen years ago. It had been six months since I'd seen it last, and my skin was practically itching to touch the nylon again.

Only once, after the police told us what they'd found in Stefan De Luca's truck, had I checked to make sure mine was still there. And it was. I had no idea how that cop got his hands on an identical bag or rope, but my bag was still safely in its place.

Perhaps he was a copycat.

He'd have all the case information from my crimes, after all. Never enough to catch me, of course. I'd always been too careful. I was an overthinker. I weighed every option, played out variations of each scenario before I acted. I'd never left DNA behind, never chosen similar women, didn't kill every victim, and never followed a pattern or timeline. I let it happen when the mood struck, but I was prepared for anything.

The only person who'd ever known who I truly was happened to be Seth. And I'd bought his silence the way he'd asked for it, by bending him over the edge of his bed. If Glennon hadn't caught us that day, I was sure it would've had to continue. Not that I minded, I guessed. Seth was a good fuck. But I much preferred women.

Then.

I much preferred women *then.*

I only preferred my wife now.

I twisted the pearl bracelet around my fingers. I hadn't taken Illiana De Luca's underwear because I hadn't raped her. I hated her too much for that. I hated that she got to come into my secret space.

Throughout the years, I'd only brought the most special women down here—the ones I wanted to have a bit of extra fun with. There were fifteen in total that had died in this room. Fifteen beautiful bodies I'd buried in our woods. If Ainsley would've let me, Stefan would've joined them. But she'd fought it. She thought it was too risky, and I could never tell her why it wasn't.

It was only fitting that now, Illiana was buried with Stefan, concrete setting mere feet above their heads at that very moment. The only thing I wanted to do was end her life, and I had. But still, I wanted a token. Illiana's bracelet was the perfect way to remember her. Touching it now, I remembered slipping it off her wrist as I tossed her body into the freezer, ending our problems once and for all. I'd waited until Ainsley had gone to bed that night, then moved her body from my trunk to the freezer without my wife ever suspecting a thing.

She believed me when I'd said I went out for a drive to clear my head. And, I knew if the police were to ever ask, Mallory and Gina could account for my time half of the night. Truth was, I'd gone to see Mallory because I'd had an urge that night. I needed clarity, and I had the clearest mind when I was ending a life. If Gina hadn't been there, it might've been Mallory's underwear I was putting in my special bag. Oh, what fun that would've been.

Instead, I'd gone after Illiana, which worked out better in the end anyway. Gina talked sense into me. She told me I needed to take matters into my own hands, and that was what I'd done. I'd solved our worries, made sure Illiana wasn't a problem, and satisfied my urges all in one night. Thanks to me, Stefan would never hurt my wife. Thanks to me, Illiana would never bother us again. Thanks to my wife, this would be the last item I'd ever put into the bag.

I was done.

A changed man.

Maybe. Probably.

I reached for the zipper, unzipping the bag in a hurry, ready to tuck it back away before Ainsley came out to see what was taking so long. As I pulled it open, I froze.

No.

No.

No. No. No. No.

NoNoNoNoNoNoNoNO.

My stomach twisted into a knot. The bag was nearly empty. No underwear. No rope. Only a single, white envelope with tape and her signature over the seal.

She'd set the cop up.

She'd known all along.

I pulled the envelope out of the bag with shaking hands and tore it open, letting the note inside fall out. As I read it, I felt the vomit rising in my throat.

Sorry, honey.
Rules are rules.
No more secrets.

ENJOYED THE ARRANGEMENT?

If you enjoyed this story, please consider leaving me a quick review. It doesn't have to be long—just a few words will do. Who knows? Your review might be the thing that encourages a future reader to take a chance on my work!
To leave a review, please visit:
mybook.to/arrangement

Let everyone know how much you loved
The Arrangement on Goodreads:
http://bit.ly/383z5hb

DON'T MISS THE NEXT RELEASE FROM KIERSTEN MODGLIN!

Thank you so much for reading this story. I'd love to invite you to sign up for my mailing list and text alerts so we can be sure you don't miss my next release.

Sign up for my mailing list here:
http://eepurl.com/dhiRRv
Sign up for my text alerts here:
www.kierstenmodglinauthor.com/textalerts.html

ACKNOWLEDGMENTS

First and foremost, to my amazing husband and beautiful little girl, thank you for believing in me when this was all just a dream and for helping me to make it a reality. I love you both more than life.

To my friend, Emerald O'Brien, thank you for being my biggest cheerleader, my sounding board, and the one with tough love when things just aren't working. I'm so grateful for your friendship and support.

To my immensely talented editor, Sarah West, thank you for seeing the story through the chaos. I'm forever grateful to have you on my team.

To the proofreading team at My Brother's Editor, thank you for your eagle eyes and ability to spot the most stubborn typos. I'm so thankful to work with you!

To my loyal readers—thank you for believing in me. Thank you for celebrating every release, for following me in whatever direction I decide to go, and for loving my stories as much as I do. I'm so honored to get to spend my life bringing you stories. Your support means the absolute world to me and I truly couldn't do this without you.

Last but certainly not least, to you—the person reading this book. Thank you for supporting art and for being a reader. I hope you've enjoyed this wild journey. Whether this was your first Kiersten Modglin novel or your twenty-second, I hope it was everything you hoped for and nothing like you expected.

ABOUT THE AUTHOR

Kiersten Modglin is an Amazon Top 30 bestselling author of award-winning psychological suspense novels and a member of International Thriller Writers. Kiersten lives in Nashville, Tennessee with her husband, daughter, and their two Boston Terriers: Cedric and Georgie. She is best known for her unpredictable suspense and her readers have dubbed her 'The Queen of Twists.' A Netflix addict, Shonda Rhimes super-fan, psychology fanatic, and indoor enthusiast, Kiersten enjoys rainy days spent with her nose in a book.

Sign up for Kiersten's newsletter here:
http://eepurl.com/b3cNFP
Sign up for text alerts from Kiersten here:
www.kierstenmodglinauthor.com/textalerts.html

www.kierstenmodglinauthor.com

ALSO BY KIERSTEN MODGLIN

STANDALONE NOVELS

Becoming Mrs. Abbott

The List

The Missing Piece

Playing Jenna

The Beginning After

The Better Choice

The Good Neighbors

The Lucky Ones

I Said Yes

The Mother-in-Law

The Dream Job

The Liar's Wife

My Husband's Secret

The Perfect Getaway

The Roommate

The Missing

Just Married

THE MESSES SERIES

The Cleaner (The Messes, #1)

The Healer (The Messes, #2)

The Liar (The Messes, #3)

The Prisoner (The Messes, #4)

NOVELLAS

The Long Route: A Lover's Landing Novella

The Stranger in the Woods: A Crimson Falls Novella

THE LOCKE INDUSTRIES SERIES

The Nanny's Secret

CPSIA information can be obtained
at www.ICGtesting.com
Printed in the USA
LVHW112049060621
689488LV00005B/929

9 798599 706618